I kept the nine-millimeter on him, but I didn't make a big thing of it. He had decided to try and talk his way out of this, and I wanted to encourage that view. But I watched him. Close.

"You mind if I smoke?" he asked, sitting on the couch beneath the open stairway to the loft.

"I don't mind," I said.

"You got any cigarettes around this joint, then?"

"No."

"No?"

"I don't smoke myself, and I don't keep cigarettes in my house."

"Why not, for Christsake?"

"They're bad for you."

He thought that was funny, or pretended to. He laughed and shook his head for thirty seconds and said, "You got anything to drink?"

"Coke, Dr. Pepper, Seven-Up."

"And what else?"

"I got some wine, but I'm saving that for New Year's Eve."

That tickled him, too, or anyway he laughed about it. "Shit, man, you live like a fuckin' nun."

"Monk."

"Whatever. But that's how you live. If you call this living."

"It beats what your partner's doing."

That stopped him, for just a moment, and he said, "You been waiting for this, haven't you? You were ready for us."

"Either that," I said, "or you weren't ready for me..."

HARD CASE CRIME BOOKS
BY MAX ALLAN COLLINS:

QUARRY
QUARRY'S LIST
QUARRY'S DEAL
QUARRY'S CUT
QUARRY'S VOTE
THE LAST QUARRY
THE FIRST QUARRY
QUARRY IN THE MIDDLE
QUARRY'S EX
THE WRONG QUARRY
QUARRY'S CHOICE
DEADLY BELOVED
SEDUCTION OF THE INNOCENT
TWO FOR THE MONEY
THE CONSUMMATA *(with Mickey Spillane)*

QUARRY'S LIST

by **Max Allan Collins**

A HARD CASE CRIME NOVEL

A HARD CASE CRIME BOOK
(HCC-so3)
First Hard Case Crime edition: October 2015

Published by

Titan Books
A division of Titan Publishing Group Ltd
144 Southwark Street
London SE1 0UP

in collaboration with Winterfall LLC

Cover painting by Robert McGinnis

Print edition ISBN 978-1-78329-885-3
E-book ISBN 978-1-78329-886-0

Design direction by Max Phillips
www.maxphillips.net

Typeset by Swordsmith Productions

Printed in the United States of America

Visit us on the web at www.HardCaseCrime.com

*You know, I thought it would be hard to find
the right words to dedicate a book
to MICKEY SPILLANE
—but it wasn't.
It was easy.*

"He's makin' a list, checkin' it twice..."
Santa Claus is Coming to Town

QUARRY'S LIST

1

A noise woke me.

Not much of a noise, but enough of one to tell me I wasn't alone in the house. The convincing thing was the dead silence that followed that little bump-in-the-night, an unnatural silence, and I found myself holding my breath, much as the intruder downstairs must have been.

I sat up in bed, leaned over toward the window, parted the curtains, and looked out. Looked down. It had snowed today, the season's first snowfall; and the cold late November day had turned into a dark, even colder night. The ground was covered with a good five inches of white, and the footprints showed.

That was when I first consciously realized the .38 was in my hand. I'd been keeping the gun under the pillow on the side of the bed that hadn't been getting much use lately. Neither had the gun, outside of my carrying it around with me all the time, like some sort of goddamn .38-caliber security blanket.

But all blankets were tossed aside now, and I was sitting up in bed, and the gun in my hand wasn't a symbol anymore, not just something to make me feel comfortable. No.

It was something to kill people with.

People like the two men who were invading my lake home at this very moment. Right now there was only one of them in the house, but another man was outside, backing the first guy up. No doubt of that. That was standard, a team of two, but that didn't bother me. They wouldn't be coming in together.

Which was nice, because it's easier to kill people one at a time. Two-on-one may be okay in basketball, but not in this game.

I didn't make any noise getting out of bed. Three and a half months of practice had made me good. The guy downstairs was good, too, I supposed, but he wasn't *that* good; he hadn't lived here like I had, he didn't know this place other than maybe from photographs or an afternoon prowl he and his partner may have made sometime when I was away. And I'm always gone in the afternoon. So it would have been easy.

Easy to get in and look around, yes; but that wouldn't make it easy to invade the place in the middle of an overcast, moonless, colder-than-fuck night. Not without making a noise, anyway.

And, too, I was ready for visitors. Oh, nothing elaborate. No alarm system or any of that bullshit. An alarm system isn't going to do any good if the man who wants to come inside knows what he's doing. Even a good amateur can get around an alarm. And a professional, a thief, say, or a hitman like the one downstairs, wouldn't be stopped by anything but an outrageously elaborate, expensive system with triple backups and the works. I didn't have the money or the patience for that and of course most of the more effective alarm systems are arranged to trigger a light on a panel at some police station, and I didn't exactly want to explain to any police why it was I needed an alarm in my house.

But I did have a system. Not an alarm system; nothing more than my own built-in alarm, which comes from those rice-paddy warfare years I suffered through, where you learned to sleep light unless you didn't care about waking up. The best warning system depends not on electronics, but on devious thinking. You have to be smarter than the guy trying to break in. That comes from Vietnam, too, I guess: the tendency to think of psychological and even guerilla warfare rather than more conventional, unimaginative means.

The layout of my little A-frame cottage is simple: two bedrooms in the rear, one of which is clearly the master bedroom (twice as large as the adjacent spare, and with triple the closet space); a small bathroom next to the master bedroom, across from the laundry room; a big open living-room area, with a kitchenette on the left, as you come into the room from the hallway along which are the bedrooms, bath, and laundry rooms; and an open loft dominated by an oversize couch. The couch converts into a double-size bed at night.

Both bedrooms downstairs have easy-access windows, and the footprints I'd seen had led to both of those windows, so I couldn't be sure which bedroom he'd decided to enter. If my second-guessing of the intruder's strategy was right, he'd have come in the window of the spare bedroom, the one that seemed not to be in use; but he may have been second-guessing me, and might have figured I'd use the spare bedroom to throw him off.

Whichever way he'd used to come in, he was by now surely finding out that the lumpish shape under the covers in the master bedroom's bed was three pillows and not a body. In fact, if I listened real close, I might be able to pinpoint the exact moment when...

And I heard the thud.

I smiled.

There are a number of sounds in the world that can be described by the word "thud," but there is only one sound like the thud that comes from a silenced automatic. And that thud had just sounded in the bedroom downstairs, right below me.

I had him. He was dead. Technically alive, yes, breathing. But dead.

The trick was, since another guy was outside, I probably should kill the one downstairs with his own gun. My .38 was not silenced (as no silencer made can truly silence a revolver, with its exposed chamber) and if I fired it at him, the noise would probably scare away his friend outside.

And I didn't want him scared away.

I wanted him curious.

I wanted him to come in and say hello.

I wondered what the best way would be to get the silenced automatic away from the guy below. I don't like to kill people with my hands; I'm not into that. Strangling people, breaking necks, snapping spines, you can have it.

But it looked like any way I figured it, some sort of struggle was going to be inevitable. Now, I'm not exactly a bruiser; I'm a couple inches under six foot, and at one hundred sixty pounds I was heavier than I'd been in a long time. I'm also no expert in karate or any of that; the only belt I wear holds my pants up. I know the basics of hand-to-hand, from Marine training; but from practical experience I've found that whenever I'm in a kill-or-be-killed situation, pulling a trigger is all the exercise I crave.

On the other hand, there are certain situations where a certain amount of physical violence can't be avoided.

When the guy below me stepped out of the hallway and into the open, I jumped down from the loft and landed with both feet on his shoulders.

The air gushed out of him, but he didn't have a chance to say anything before he was unconscious. He hit the floor limp, like a fat man rolling out of bed, and I came down on top of him, using him to cushion my own fall. The silenced automatic tumbled from his fingers. I picked it up.

A nine-millimeter automatic. Like the one I used to use. I had to smile. The sensation of the nine-millimeter in my hand was not an altogether unpleasant experience. It was almost like shaking hands with an old friend.

On the floor, the guy was starting to rouse.

There were no lights on, of course, so I couldn't see much of him. He was my size, about, a little heavier maybe.

He was wearing black: heavy turtleneck sweater, slacks, even the stocking cap pulled down over his ears. His cheeks were red, against otherwise pale, pale skin.

And now he was up into a sitting position, there on the floor, his eyes open, and before he could say a word I said, "Take off your clothes."

He didn't say, "What?"

He didn't say anything. He was a pro. He just started taking off his clothes, sweater first. The ribbing of thermal underwear was revealed as the sweater gave way. I didn't blame him for the long johns. It was cold out there.

"Just down to your underwear," I said.

He nodded, piled the sweater and slacks and stocking cap on the nearby kitchenette counter. "Shoes and socks, too," I said.

He shrugged and started to unlace his black military-style boots.

"I don't have to tell you not to try throwing a shoe at me or anything, do I? No, I didn't think so."

He put the boots on the counter, and sighed, as if to say, "What now?"

"Back to the bedroom," I said.

He started walking down the hallway. When we got to the end, he veered toward the master bedroom.

"No," I said. "The other one."

I wanted him to use the spare bedroom, because I had new sheets on the other bed, and the bed in here just had some old ragged ones I wouldn't mind messing up. Also, there was a plastic liner.

"Get in," I said, motioning to the bed.

He hesitated, showing confusion and, for the first time, worry.

"Don't screw it up now," I said. "You been fine up to here. Very professional. I respect that. So do as I say, and maybe you'll be around tomorrow. Get in bed."

Reluctantly, he climbed under the covers. There was more light in here, as the drapes were back and the light from the street a quarter-mile over was seeping in. I saw his face: young, rather blank, his features very ordinary but not unpleasant. His skin was extremely pale, the cold-reddened cheeks fading now.

"Pull the covers up around your neck," I said. He did.

"Now what?" he said, speaking for the first time.

And the last.

The silenced nine-millimeter made its thudding sound and I went back out into the living room to get into the dead man's clothes.

2

I sat on the floor in the spare bedroom with my back against the dresser and played dead. The second guy would be coming in sometime within the next five to ten minutes and, hopefully, would in the darkness assume the figure dressed in black, slumped on the bedroom floor, was his partner; and that the blood-spattered shape in the bed was me.

I didn't have to fool him forever; all I wanted was a second. One second for him to be confused, seeing things not as they were but as I wanted them seen. One second, and I could take him without a struggle.

It would have been easier, of course, to just shoot him. But I couldn't do that. Not and kill him, anyway. I could have shot him in the arm or leg, I suppose, but that wouldn't necessarily incapacitate him. Some people can put up a pretty good fight, despite a wound. Some people can even be more dangerous wounded than not; getting shot pisses them off, and the next time you shoot it better be to kill.

And killing was out of the question, at this point, at least. I had to talk to this guy, which is why I wanted to avoid any extended struggle with him. In a struggle, people can get hurt. They can even get killed. And like I said, I had to talk to this guy, and if one of us was dead, talking would be pretty well ruled out.

That was where all of my precautions, all my strategy had begun. Three and a half months ago I had tried to burn some bridges behind me, but I knew the possibility existed of a bridge or two surviving my incendiary efforts. And if such was the case, someone—I didn't know who, exactly, but someone—would decide to have me hit. The contract would very probably be handled by a team of two; one would carry out the hit itself, the other would be the backup man. From the very beginning I had known the best way to handle that eventuality would be to kill the first man in, and then wait for the backup man, who, seeing his partner dead, might be persuaded to give me certain information.

Precisely what that information would be, I couldn't say. I hoped for the name of the man who had hired the two killers, but that was a slim hope. Most likely the assignment had been through somebody like the Broker. But with the Broker dead, some other middleman would be involved, and if I could get the middleman's name, it would be an easy step to the name I really wanted.

So I was prepared for the invasion of my home by men sent to kill me. I had almost been looking forward to it, as until an attempt was made on my life, or until sufficient time had passed—say three years—without any such attempt, my life would be in limbo. And I didn't have the funds to maintain a three-year vacation. Or the patience. The cottage had been my home for five years, and I always had enjoyed my quiet, lakeside existence. But that had been when I was working, when I was gone for a week or more on a job, and then would come back for rest and solitude. Year-round rest and solitude, though, could prove boring and probably stagnating. And, in the past, I'd spent a lot of time enjoying myself, with friends (a regular group of us played poker, sometimes as often as three nights a week), and at nearby Lake Geneva, primarily at the Playboy Club. This was a vacation area, with water sports in the summer, skiing in the winter, so there were good-looking women to be had most of the time.

But all of that I'd had to put on the shelf. With the possibility of an attempt on my life coming at any given moment, I couldn't allow myself the luxury of being distracted. And my poker-playing pals, who were straight types who thought I was a lingerie salesman, might get a little unnerved if our game got broken up one night by gunfire. My sex life had to be forgone, if for no other reason than it's hard to keep it up when any second you might get shot down. And, too, you tend to be somewhat off your guard when you're fucking somebody. People have been killed in bed before, it happens all the time, and dying happy is some small compensation, I guess, but no thank you.

All of my attention, then, had been focused on my survival in this specific situation: the invasion of my home by killers. And my biggest worry right now, as I sat slumped on the floor in the spare bedroom, in the company of a man I'd just killed, was that I had overtrained. Not so much in the sense of an athlete who leaves his best game on the practice field; but that I had gone overboard, had devised a paranoid's plan, and not that of a realist. Had I been too elaborate? I couldn't help feeling like a silly ass, sitting there playing dead, dressed up in somebody else's clothes, waiting to point my gun and say, "Trick or treat!"

In the late summer and fall afternoons, when I would sit on my porch studying the shimmer of the lake, watching the leaves turn gold, sipping a bottle of soda (I'm not a beer drinker) and daydreaming about my eventual triumph over the killers who would, one day, one night, invade my lakeside sanctuary, my preparations had seemed sane and necessary. Now, in early winter, the day of the first snow, sitting on the cold floor of the spare bedroom, sharing that bedroom with a dead man, wearing his clothes, pretending to be dead myself, I wasn't sure.

However I figured it, the second guy would be harder to take. He'd be coming into a situation he assumed had gone wrong. That's what working backup is all about. Your partner's late getting back, and you figure something must have got fucked up, and you go in to see what.

If I could have counted on him coming in the same way as his partner, through the window just to my left here in the spare bedroom, all I would have had to do was stand to one side and stick a gun in his ribs as he stepped over the sill. No problem. No struggle.

But he wouldn't come in the same window. He wouldn't be coming in at all if something hadn't gone wrong. His partner had, obviously, made at least one mistake. Going in the same way could mean stepping in the same pile of dog shit as his partner. So the window was out. That much I could count on. That, and that he would be coming in. Somehow.

In the meantime, I waited.

Sharing a room with a dead man can be a less than pleasant experience, especially if the man's bowels empty when he dies, as is common. All of a sudden you begin to understand how the tradition of flowers at funerals got started. But this corpse had better manners than most, and wasn't smelling up the room at all. He was, in fact, better company than a lot of people I've met.

The only bad thing about him was he was a size smaller than me, and his clothes made a tight, slightly uncomfortable fit. But I did have the silenced nine-millimeter to thank him for, so what the hell. You can't have everything.

I was just wondering if I could get away with clearing my throat when I realized I wasn't alone.

I'd expected him to be good, but this was ridiculous. He was a few feet away from me before I even knew he was inside. The second guy, I mean, not the corpse. The corpse was staying put. But his partner was inching silently toward the spare bedroom, moving down the hall like something floating. He must have come in through the living room, which was damn near impossible. The door in there creaked, and the only way to open the windows from the outside was with a screwdriver or maybe a crowbar; and once open, the windows led in over all sorts of furniture, which would in turn lead to making all sorts of noise.

But there had been no noise, and I was so surprised to sense him approaching, I almost moved.

He stooped down to me. Touched my shoulder with his left hand. His right hand had a gun in it. "Beatty?" he said.

I grabbed his right hand and shook the gun loose. I nudged his belly with the nine-millimeter. "Up," I said.

We stood together. Slowly. His gun on the floor, mine in his gut.

"You must be Quarry," he said.

3

I flicked on the light switch with my free hand and got a look at the guy. He, too, was dressed in black; he wore a quilted thermal jacket instead of a sweater, but basically we were dressed the same, and stood there facing each other like a reflection.

He was smaller than me, at least an inch or two shorter, though by weight he was a little heavier, I'd imagine, but not softer. His brown hair was thin on top, trimmed close on the sides, and he had the friendly face of a bartender who can be your buddy all night long, then the second you step out of line, whip a sash weight from under the bar and split your head open.

"The jacket," I said.

He made a shrugging smile and unzipped the jacket and got out of it slowly and let it drop. He watched my eyes to see if they followed the jacket. They didn't.

He wore a red, black, and white plaid shirt, a hunter's shirt. There was no holster, shoulder or otherwise. His silenced automatic, the nine-millimeter's twin, which I'd already kicked over in the corner, was more than a holster could handle, except for perhaps something special made. But then a hitman usually has little need to constantly carry a gun, would only carry a gun those few minutes it

takes to get a job done, so the lack of a holster was no surprise.

"The wall," I said.

He nodded and slowly turned to the side wall, leaned
against it in the space between the closet and the door,
hands behind his head, legs spread.

I patted him down. I felt a hard narrow shaft as my
hand traveled over his left trouser pocket, which either
meant he was horny or he had a knife in there. I ripped
the pocket open and a stiletto hit the floor.

"Cute," I said.

"Some people don't like knives," he said pleasantly,
glancing back over his shoulder at me. "Me, I don't mind
'em. I'm not squeamish."

His voice was medium-pitched, well-modulated. It
went well with his friendly bartender face.

I kicked his knife over toward the corner, and it bounced
off the wall and ended up under the bed. "Okay," I said.
"Stand away."

He released his hands from their behind-the-head
clasp, turned around, and looked over toward his dead
partner. We were in close, because the room was very
small, sort of a closet with aspirations. I didn't like the
closeness, because this guy was obviously stronger than
me, and his carrying a knife indicated he was less wary of
physical struggle than I am. Also, anyone who carries a
knife—that is, anyone who carries a knife expressly to kill
people—has psychotic tendencies, if you ask me. At the
very least, such a person reveals a disturbing willingness
to make a mess.

So I tried to keep a few feet between us, which was a challenge in that tiny room.

"You mind if I take a look?" he asked, gesturing toward the bed.

"Go right ahead."

He lifted the sheet back and looked at his partner. I looked at him. I figured he was hoping I'd look at his partner, but I'm afraid I disappointed him. He let the sheet drop, shook his head, said, "Just had the little bastard broke in."

"That's a shame."

"I guess I should've taught him a little better. Shit. He must've come in like the fourth of fuckin' July."

"That's right."

"I told him this was a special case. Little bastard's been getting cocky lately, and just wouldn't listen. Guess this'll teach him."

"I guess."

"You know, this here was very good, exchanging clothes with my boy Beatty here, you fooled me good."

"Maybe you been getting cocky lately."

"Yeah!" the guy laughed. "Maybe I have at that. Look, Quarry…you mind I call you Quarry?"

"Be my guest."

"I'm Lynch. I'd offer you a hand to shake, but…"

"I understand."

"Well, anyway. Looks like we got a situation here, don't we?"

"Looks like it."

"Could we get out of this cramped bedroom? I just

know you're not going to be comfortable talking to me till we do."

I nodded. "The living room. You know the way. You came in through there."

"I did at that. It was a tricky fucker, too. You want me to turn on the hall switch?"

"Know where it is, do you?"

"Fuck, yes. I been in here three times."

"Really? I'd have thought you were good enough to get by on once."

He laughed. "We better stop tryin' to impress each other and go in the other room and talk like civilized people."

"Good idea," I said, and we did.

I kept the nine-millimeter on him, but I didn't make a big thing of it. He had decided to try and talk his way out of this, and I wanted to encourage that view. But I watched him. Close.

"You mind if I smoke?" he asked, sitting on the couch beneath the open stairway to the loft.

I had pulled the kitchen stool around and was sitting on that. I liked being up a shade higher than him.

"I don't mind," I said.

"You got any cigarettes around this joint, then? I didn't bring mine in with me."

"No."

"No?"

"I don't smoke myself, and I don't keep cigarettes in my house."

"Why not, for Christsake?"

"They're bad for you."

He thought that was funny, or pretended to. He laughed and shook his head for thirty seconds and said, "You got anything to drink?"

"Coke, Dr. Pepper, Seven-Up."

"And what else?"

"I got some wine, but I'm saving that for New Year's Eve."

That tickled him, too, or anyway he laughed about it. "Shit, man, you live like a fuckin' nun."

"Monk."

"Whatever. But that's how you live. If you call this living."

"It beats what your partner's doing."

That stopped him, for just a moment, and he said, "You been waiting for this, haven't you? You were ready for us."

"Either that," I said, "or you weren't ready for me."

"Ain't that the truth, pal. Ain't it the truth. But you ought to be crazy by now. How long has it been like this? No booze, no friends, no women, just cooped up here."

"I get out once a day."

"Sure. You go swimming over at the Y at Lake Geneva. Some fun."

"Be grateful. If I didn't go swimming every day, you wouldn't ever have got in here to look around."

"Yeah, and fuck of a lot of good it did us."

"You're still alive."

"For how long?"

"That's up to you."

"Is it? I'd like to think so, but you seem to have a gun in your hand, and my boy Beatty seems to be shot to shit in the other room."

"But you aren't."

"Yeah, well, not yet, but maybe pretty soon, huh?"

"Maybe."

"So it boils down to this, Quarry, right? I got something you want…a name. And you got something I want…my life. So. Can we work a trade?"

"Why not?"

"Why not, he asks. You're holding 'why not' in your fuckin' hand, and you know it. I can give you the name you want, but there's no guarantee you'll give me my life, if I do. Not that I don't trust you, but there just isn't any guarantee."

"There's no guarantee you'll give me the right name, either, so we just have to trust each other, I guess."

"You could look at it that way. I don't. I think we got what you call your typical Mexican standoff here, and seems to me we ought to look for some alternate route around this, what you call, impasse we're at."

"I'm listening."

"I'm glad…'cause I just happen to have an alternate route in mind."

"I'm still listening."

"I'm still glad. I'm glad we're getting along so good, too, 'cause my alternate route is this: throw in together."

"And do what?"

"Hey, you're supposed to be listening. Just keep listening, and when you hear what I got to say, you'll understand what I mean. And, Quarry, I'm going to prove to you just how sincere I really am, man. I'm going to give you your fuckin' name. That's the main thing you're after, right? I'll give you the fucker, no strings attached, and then I'll explain how we're going to throw in together and make us a pile. Interested?"

This time I laughed.

"Okay," I said. "So what's the name?"

4

Vietnam taught me a lot of things, but coming home taught me more. The beginning of my education was finding my wife in bed with a guy named Williams. The only reason I didn't shoot Williams on the spot was I didn't have a gun on me, and he was too big to slug it out with, so I ended up backing out of there, feeling embarrassed, somehow, for having interrupted.

The next morning, after I'd cooled down and thought the situation over in the rational light of day, I went out to Williams's bungalow in La Mirada, where I found him on his back in his driveway, working on the rear end of his little sportscar, which was jacked up with the back wheels off. He looked up at me and said, "I got nothing to say to you, bunghole," and I said fine and kicked out the jack.

I didn't kill my wife. Had she been under the car at the time, I would have dropped it on her just as fast as Williams. But she wasn't, and any feeling I had for her died with her boyfriend. She divorced me, of course. I couldn't have cared less.

They gave it a lot of play in the papers, but there was no trial. No district attorney in his right mind would bother trying a case like that. Even in an unpopular war, the returning warrior has the right to get upset when he finds his wife fucking somebody. In fact, those two situations seem to be the socially sanctioned situations for killing people: war, and when you find your wife fucking somebody.

On the other hand, I couldn't find work. Everybody sympathized with me, didn't blame me a bit for what I'd done, and told me so in no uncertain terms. I got more sympathy than a terminal cancer patient. And about as many job offers.

Before I went in the service, I worked in a garage, but everywhere I went I was told there were no openings for a mechanic, which I knew wasn't entirely accurate, as Williams had been a mechanic, too, so the job market was short at least one. The publicity about my homecoming was obviously working against me, but there was also a general negative attitude toward hiring Vietnam veterans, since a lot of employers assumed we were all dope addicts.

I spent a lonely month in L.A., feeling sorry for myself, drinking, and trying to catch V.D. California itself was enough to bring me down. The place was full of bad memories, or rather good memories that had gone bad, as this was where I'd been stationed before going over, where I'd met my California girl, my bride with the sun-bleached brown hair and golden tan and lush figure just made for a bikini, an image in my memory that had turned dark and brittle, like newspaper left out in the sun.

The first week my old man came out to see me and tell me not to come home. Home was Ohio, and a stepmother who thought me strange even before I started dropping cars on people. My old man hadn't needed bother to come tell me not to go home, but his doing so didn't particularly help my mental state.

Neither did his insistence that my "murder" of Williams didn't bother him, because it was offset by all the good things I'd done in the service of my country. By good things he meant all those yellow people I killed.

After a while I began getting tired of counting the cockroaches on the walls of my "apartment," two rooms, one of which was the toilet. Besides, I was broke. I knew I'd have to get off my butt and find something to keep myself going. And while I had learned in Vietnam about the meaninglessness of life and death—a view that had only been reinforced since my return to the states—I'd also had instilled in me the importance of survival. Those two views should be incompatible, I suppose, but they aren't. Anyone who's been in a war can tell you it's quite possible to believe in survival while placing no value in life and death.

I never asked the Broker how he got my name, although it seems obvious enough to me now that he'd seen about me in the papers, and saw some potential in me, perhaps even was able to anticipate my weeks of unsuccessful job-hunting, and my month of cheap booze and cheaper hookers. Anyway, he knew where to find me. He came right to my two-room suite at the Fleabag Hilton and made his pitch.

Funny thing, I can't remember the conversation. I can remember my surprise, answering the knock at the door, expecting the landlord come to bitch about next week's rent, and finding instead the dignified-looking, white-haired gentleman, with the neatly trimmed mustache, conservative but well-cut gray suit, and general demeanor of a successful lawyer or politician. He also had that ambiguity of age his type often has: he appeared to be around forty, though I later learned he was nearer fifty than forty; as long as I knew him, he looked a good ten years younger than he really was despite the stark white hair. I think it was the lack of lines in that long face of his.

I remember my surprise at seeing this distinguished apparition at the door of the trash can I was living in, but the conversation that followed I can't summon up. I remember it in substance, but not detail.

I know he didn't come right out and ask me if I wanted to kill people for money. He was much more subtle than that. He did it all with implication, in that eloquently long-winded politician's way of his, telling me without really saying it that I could make a lot of money doing what I had done overseas for very little money. I had already shown, in the case of the late Mr. Williams, my willingness to kill for free. Now I was being tested to find if I had any aversion to doing the same for a fee.

I was at a point in my life where I could have gone in any direction; all I needed was a push. If somebody religious had got hold of me, he could've made a missionary out of me.

But somebody religious didn't come around.

The Broker did.

5

"Ash," he said.

"What?"

"That's the name. Mean anything to you?"

"No."

"Good. Because I just happen to have an address that goes with it. That, you can have later on."

"Later on."

"Right. Soon as we get some trust built up in each other. You can understand that, can't you?"

"I can understand that. You want to tell me about Ash?"

"He worked through the Broker. Like you. Like me. Like that dead kid in bed in the other room."

"So he worked through the Broker. So what?"

"So three and a half months ago, the Broker was killed. Or, should I say, hit."

"No kidding."

"And I think we both know who hit him."

"Do we?"

"Come on, Quarry. You killed the Broker. Don't fuck around."

"What if I didn't?"

"Kill the Broker, you mean? Wouldn't matter. Ash thinks you did."

"Don't stop now. You're rolling."

"I kind of thought you'd find this interesting. Anyway, Ash, or somebody behind him, wants to take over where the Broker left off. And figures doing away with the guy that killed the Broker is a necessary safety precaution for anybody planning to step in the Broker's shoes."

"When do you get to the part where you and me make a pile?"

"I'm there already. All we got to do, Quarry, is ease Ash out. Or, Ash and whoever's behind him, if there is somebody behind him. That part I'm not sure about, but it's no problem."

"Then what?"

"Then we, Quarry, *we* take over for the Broker. We play the middleman role and get some of the safe money, for a change. Shit! Who in fuck is better qualified than us?"

I nodded. Sat staring thoughtfully at him.

"I know, I know," he said. "There's more to it than just what I've said. I'm just sketching it in, broad strokes, broad strokes. But it's not hard to see that there's more here than just one man can handle. Two men...if they're men like you and me, Quarry, the sky's the fuckin' limit, man. What do you say?"

"How about 'this is so sudden'?"

"Take your time. Think it over. Nobody's rushing you."

"You keep talking. I'll be thinking it over."

"Okay. First move is, hit Ash. Got to question him first, of course, find out if this was his idea, and if not, whose it was. We got to find out about the mechanical side, too, you know, find out just how exactly taking over Broker's old setup could be put into effect. I mean, I assume there's a list or something of the people like you and me who worked through the Broker, and we'll need that; that'll be the key. Questioning Ash won't be any big deal. I, uh, know how to get people to talk to me, if I have to. Even somebody like Ash."

I remembered the stiletto in the other room and knew what he meant.

"All right. I gave you the name, like I said, But it's meaningless without the address. I can take you there. We can go see Ash together, we could go tonight."

"It's within driving distance, then?"

"That's right. You'll excuse me for not being exact about how far, or how long it'll take us, you understand. But if we left now, we could be there in...a reasonable amount of time, yes."

"You do realize there's a body in the other room that needs getting rid of."

"Oh, well, sure. No problem. We could do that on the way."

We wrapped the body in the bedclothing; the plastic cover I'd put on the bed was dark green, and not only held in the mess, but made for a nice dark bundle that would look relatively inconspicuous, should we happen to be seen depositing it in the back of his station wagon. The wagon was parked beyond the bushes that separated my property from the road. I am on the outskirts of a town of less than one hundred population, so the road is lit, but not particularly well traveled, especially in winter, in the early predawn hours.

There are a lot of sand and gravel pits along the Wisconsin and Illinois border. The greatest number are near Woodstock, which is thirty or so miles from my cottage. The abandoned pits fill with water, and there was one of those, a large one, a mile and a half from me. In the summer the tree-encircled, water-filled pit is used by kids of various ages for skinny dipping. In the winter it isn't used for much of anything.

Around a year ago August some teenagers were swimming there and some kid with good lungs went tooling way down underwater to see what he could see. What he saw was a car with three bodies in it. The bodies were floating around inside, bloated, decomposing, full of bullet holes.

The authorities called it a gangland killing, which it probably was.

I didn't have to mention any of this, of course. We both knew that we were close enough to Chicago to be able to dump a shot-up corpse about anywhere and have it called a gangland killing.

He was still talking, but I wasn't listening. I had him drive, just to keep his hands busy, and interrupted him with instructions when necessary, which he followed cheerfully. We were on a gravel side road, now.

"See that little inroad, up there?" I said. "There between those two big trees?"

"I see it."

"When you get there, back in, slowly."

"Okay. You know something funny, Quarry?"

"Not that I can think of."

"I feel a little bad about that kid back there." He jerked a thumb over his shoulder toward the lump in the bed-clothes behind us.

"Really."

"I mean it. He was too young. I thought working the backup spot, after so many years of going in first, would be relaxing, but shit…with a young guy like that, no experience, impulsive, I was sitting on pins every time around, waiting to see if he pulled it off or stepped on his dick or what. No, last couple years, Broker was bringing 'em in too young. I don't think Beatty was twenty-five, even. What are you, Quarry, thirty? You must've come in young, yourself. Fuck. Must be gettin' sentimental in my old age."

"I guess I know how you feel," I said. "I lost a partner myself last year. Hey! This is it right here…don't miss it."

He started backing in, saying, "So you lost one, too, huh? Well, it happens."

"Yeah. I worked with the same partner for something like four years. Okay, whoa. This is good."

He shifted into park. "I had three different partners, since I got in the business. I guess you're my fourth."

"Yeah, well, I worked with other guys, myself. I spent a whole year, filling in where Broker needed me, whenever one half of a team wasn't available. I even worked with a guy named Ash once or twice."

He didn't catch it right away.

He was looking into the silencer by the time he said, "But I thought you said you never heard of Ash…"

"I lied," I said.

He took it between the eyes and the side of his head hit the horn. I eased him over a bit, to stop the honking, and got out of the car.

I opened the door on his side and he almost fell out. I pushed him forward so that he was prone across the seat, put the car in neutral, shut the door, got around front and pushed. A few feet from where the little inroad ended, the watery pit began.

There was a thin layer of ice that cracked open to receive the station wagon, which took only a few seconds to disappear.

I had plenty to think about on the mile-and-a-half walk back, and hardly noticed the cold.

6

The sun was out, but it seemed far away, and wasn't doing much to melt the heavy snowfall of the day before. The major streets in Milwaukee were clear, as had been the highways coming in, but many of the residential areas were still clogged with snow. Along curbs cars were surrounded by and heaped with white, their owners not even bothering to try to dig them out; homes with scooped sidewalks and driveways were few and far between. I felt lucky to find the driveway shoveled when I pulled up at the two-story house where Ash lived, or anyway where he had lived a few years ago, when I knew him.

Behind the house was a cement court which had been put in over what used to be a garden to provide parking for tenants. The big old house, with its fine Gothic lines, had been converted into an apartment house perhaps ten years ago: six apartments, four up, two down. Ash's was upstairs, with entry from the outside, here in back, the access provided by an exposed stairway and balcony that had been added onto the old house when it was changed over, a necessary measure, I supposed, but hardly a beautifying one: the staircase with balcony, and the modern-looking doors to the apartments, all but defaced the building. Which just goes to show there's more than one kind of murder people are willing to commit to make a buck.

I left my Opel GT in one of several open spaces; it was midmorning and apparently some of the tenants had gone ahead to work, despite the heavy snow. Possibly one of the remaining handful of cars belonged to Ash, but if so, I had no way of knowing which. It had been over four years since I'd seen him, and he'd have long since traded in that Thunderbird of his. Of course, I did know the name he used here, Raymond Drake, and could go peeking in the cars looking at names on registrations, if I was in the mood for making a bare-ass suspicious move like that, which I wasn't.

I got out of my car. The nine-millimeter was stuck in my belt. I was wearing an old pair of jeans and a long-sleeved sweatshirt that said Wisconsin on it and a medium-weight corduroy jacket with yellow fuzzy fur-type lining. I looked like a college kid; at least that was the object. I'm young enough looking to pass for that, I guess. On jobs I wanted to look as anonymous as possible, and my practice was to dress like a businessman, and to drive a rental car, something ordinary like a middle-price-range Ford or Chevy. But today I had my own car, my Opel GT, and it was too sporty-looking for a businessman. It could attract attention, a guy in a drab suit and trench coat stepping out of a sportscar. And attention isn't a good thing to attract when you have a nine-millimeter stuck in your belt.

I didn't have anything fancy in mind. I certainly wasn't going in shooting or kicking doors down or anything. Ash wouldn't be expecting me, or at least the possibility of that seemed slim. Of course, if my callers last night were supposed to get in touch with Ash, after killing me, he might be a little on edge, since the only way he might have heard from those guys since last night was if he'd been to a seance.

Still, I didn't figure Ash was going to be holed up in his apartment with a gun in each fist, waiting to shoot it out with me. Anyway, I hoped not. I wanted to talk to him before any shooting started. It was even possible Ash didn't live here anymore, and that some new address of his went down with that station wagon to the bottom of that gravel pit, in which case the joke was on me.

But what the hell. Sometimes a calculated risk is necessary. Once I learned Ash lived within driving distance of my cottage, I felt it safe to assume he was still living in Milwaukee, hopefully in this same apartment.

I went up the stairs. Stopped at the first door, which was not Ash's apartment. I considered knocking, to see if anybody was in there, and if nobody was, going through that apartment so I could use the hallway door to get into Ash's place. But the advantages of that were outweighed by the disadvantage of somebody possibly answering the door, and getting a good look at me, which is the reason I avoided going in the front door in the first place. After all, while I didn't necessarily plan to kill Ash, I didn't necessarily plan not to, either.

So I went on to the next, final door. Ash's door. Un-snapped my jacket. Put my right hand on the butt of the gun.

And knocked.

Nothing.

And knocked again.

Nothing.

When I tried once more and still got no response, I laid my ear against the door and listened.

Nothing. Not a damn thing.

Meaning he wasn't in there.

Probably.

Of course, if he was in there, he was being awfully silent, which meant he was dead, or waiting. And if he was waiting, waiting for me, I could be dead. In a hurry.

I took a breath. Did some thinking.

Now, I knew that Ash was like me, as far as safety pre-cautions were concerned. That is to say, he just didn't bother with them. No fancy locks or burglar alarms or anything of the sort, just his own finely honed senses. If I remembered right, there wasn't even a safety chain on the door. You could open it with a credit card.

So I did.

Very carefully, though. Once the lock clicked, I flat-tened against the side of the house, nudging the door with a foot, letting it swing open without filling the way with my own body-size target, and waited for Ash to react, if he was going to.

Nothing.

I went in low and quick, gun in hand, keeping the light from outside to my back, not easing the door shut behind me till I had a chance to scan the room, finding it empty.

Of people, that is. There was no Ash, no anyone else, but there was the clutter that was Ash. He was one of those paradoxical sorts whose professional life was the epitome of organization, and whose private life, at least as far as his surroundings were concerned, was a shambles. Ash had an orderly mind, precise, even mechanical, in the best sense of that word. But the demands of the profession evidently made him want to let loose a little when he wasn't working, when he was home; he just couldn't be bothered with a triviality like cleaning up after himself.

In other words, the place was a dump.

Not the place itself, mind you, not even the old but serviceable furniture that had come with the place. This was a dump created by the guy who lived in it. The living room, for example, looked like the aftermath of a rock festival: empty beer cans, soda cans, couple of food-encrusted paper plates, discarded newspapers, magazines, paperbacks, wadded-up paper napkins, wadded-up Kleenex, and that's all I can stand to record. The kitchen, on the other hand, wasn't as bad as you might think; there was no sink full of unwashed dishes, as Ash did no cooking for himself, outside of TV dinners, and had not lost his liking for Chinese food, as a dozen or so of the little paper carry-out containers for the stuff huddled on the counter, begging to be thrown out. The bathroom was also surprisingly clean, but that only figured. His apartment might look slovenly, but Ash himself didn't. He was well-groomed, a short, slender red-haired man with pleasant, regular features. Women liked him, and he felt the same about them. It was obvious he was between women right now—he went through them rather fast, once they found out he'd enrolled them as housekeepers first and sex objects second—and it was obvious, too, that he had left fast. Ash didn't mind living in a mess, but he didn't like coming home to one. He wouldn't have left this behind him.

But he *was* gone, and he hadn't just stepped out for a while, either. The bedroom was evidence enough of that. In addition to the expected unmade bed and general disgusting mess, I found most of his clothes gone, and there were no suitcases under the bed or in any of the closets.

I wandered out into the living room, cleared a TV dinner tray and last Sunday's newspaper off a reclining chair, and sat down. Ash was gone. The thing to do, of course, was go after him. But where had he gone? How the hell was I supposed to figure *that* one out?

There was, I supposed, an outside chance that if I sorted through the junk pile around me I might find some small indication of where he'd gone. But that was doubtful. Maybe Ash had the habit of living like a slob sometimes, but he was never a fool, and he was always a pro. And a pro can't afford to leave anything behind that could tell you where he went. Not in this line of work.

But Ash had left on apparent short notice…maybe he got sloppy this time…

And I started to laugh.

I sat and looked at the fucking mess the apartment was and said, "Yeah, maybe he got sloppy this time," and laughed some more.

And somebody knocked on the door.

"Mr. Drake?"

It was a woman's voice. Outside in the hall I'd made noise up here, was getting sloppy myself, and now I had somebody knocking on the door.

"Mr. Drake?" she said again. "Who's in there?"

I just sat in the chair, gun in my lap, waiting for her to go away. Waiting for her to decide it was just her imagination, and then once she was gone I could beat it down the back stairs to my car. But I'd be making a retreat without finding out anything, and I needed to stick around awhile and play that long shot that Ash might've left something behind that said where he went, so I got out of the chair and put the gun in my belt and went to the door and opened it.

"Hello," I said.

She was a housewife type, dressed for cleaning: an old blue work dress, hair pulled back into a bun, no makeup on at all, but not bad-looking, and probably very attractive when she wanted to be.

"Who are you?" she said.

"I'm Ray's cousin," I said.

"Cousin?"

"Hasn't Ray ever mentioned me? Charlie Wilson? He was expecting me today."

"Mr. Drake didn't say anything about expecting anyone,"

she said, looking more than a trifle suspicious and perhaps a little scared. "As a matter of fact, he left on a business trip just yesterday, and told me he wouldn't be back for some time. Possibly as long as a month. Now, could you explain why he'd be expecting you, when he was leaving?"

"No, wait," I said, smiling, hoping the smile looked real, "you got it wrong. I'm here *because* he left. He said I could use his place tonight. I came in town to check out some colleges. I just got out of service, and now I'm going back to school. Would you believe it, a guy my age?"

She drew in a breath. Then let it out. Smiled.

She bought it.

She said, "Oh, you don't look so old." She touched her face. "Now, me, I look old. It's this damn woman's work. You know. Cleaning."

"Well, this apartment could sure use it."

"I know," she smiled. "Ray doesn't keep a very tidy place, I'm afraid, does he?"

It was Ray, now; I wondered whatever happened to Mr. Drake.

"I was just coming up to clean it, when I heard you up here," she explained. "Ray asked me to get it in shape for him. He doesn't like coming home to a messy place, even though he doesn't seem to mind living in one."

"You want to come in?" I asked her.

"No, not unless you, uh…want me to clean the place up now."

"Why don't you do that this afternoon? If it's no trouble, I mean. I'll be out, then. If I get everything done I need to, I might not even have to stay the night."

"Oh, I see…well, it was nice meeting you, Mr. Wilson. I'll just leave Mr. Drake's mail and get back to my work."

And she handed me an envelope, smiled, touched her face, and left.

It was pretty obvious she and "Mr. Drake" had something going on the side. Something minor, like when her husband wasn't home and when Ash was between women; a nice fast physical fuck now and then, and probably I could have had one myself, if I'd been so inclined.

And it had been awhile since I'd been with a woman. I could've used it, I guess. But I had more urgent needs to take care of.

Though I did owe Ash's landlady some thanks.

That envelope she handed me was a motel confirmation, and it told me right where my old friend Ash had gone.

7

Before I left Milwaukee I traded my Opel GT in on a recent-model Buick, and on my way to the Quad Cities, where Ash was staying at a Holiday Inn, I got to thinking about the second of the three jobs I'd worked with him, the one where I'd saved his life.

At first glance, it was the sort of job you could pull in your sleep. We'd been provided with reams of information up front. We'd come up with a perfect, easy way to pull it off. I had the backup role and went in a week early, keeping an eye on the guy we were to hit, checking out the information we'd been given to see if the mark's schedule really was as regimented as we'd been told. And it was. The mark had a timetable he didn't vary from every working day of his life. His weekends were likewise regimented, but his working day provided that perfect, easy way I mentioned.

The mark was a real estate agent, a prosperous one. A congenial, well-dressed little man in his early fifties with a toupee and a weight problem. He had an office in the tallest building in the business district of a large Southwestern city, a hundred-thousand-dollar ranch-style house out in the country, a wife, no kids, three poodles, and mob connections.

Now, the Broker claimed not to be in the direct employ of the so-called Mafia or Family or whatever, and most of the people I helped kill had nothing to do with the mob, or, anyway, that's what I was told. But some of what those of us who worked through the Broker did was unquestionably mob related, and this supposedly fell into the area of piecework we did for them now and then, hits that for some reason or another would be better handled by outside people.

And there was no doubt that this Southwestern real estate agent had mob connections. Unless you don't consider it a little unusual for your average real estate agent to be constantly accompanied by bodyguards.

Not that they looked like bodyguards, those two guys that were always at his side. They looked like real estate agents. They were not particularly big: one of them was a sandy-haired man in his thirties who was five-eight, solid-looking but no bruiser; and the other was of similar age and height, only with brown hair, a round face, and a paunch. Neither man looked especially sinister.

But they were bodyguards, all right. No mistaking that. For instance, both of them chose to wear their suit coats at all times, even when standing out in the sun while their employer spent three hot hours one afternoon showing some of his outlying land holdings.

In the mornings they drove him to work in his yellow Cadillac. At lunch they ate at a table close by him in the restaurant on the bottom floor of his office building; they even went in with him when he used a public toilet. And in the late afternoon they drove him back to his house in the country, where their employer provided them quarters over the four-car garage. The weekends had them playing golf with him, among other things, but never mind.

The point is, they accompanied him constantly.

Except for his long lunch hours, Tuesdays and Thursdays, when he spent 12:30 to 2:30 P.M. in a sleazy little room at the Tuck-a-Way Motel, in the company of a sleazy little blonde, while the bodyguards went across the street to have lunch at a sleazy little diner.

And that, of course, was the perfect, easy way of hitting him.

The girl would be no trouble. Just shove her out of the way before the shooting started, knock her out if she got physical or vocal or anything. It would mean Ash had to pull on a stocking mask or something before going in the back window of the room and doing his thing, and he'd have to take the time to tie the girl up and gag her before cutting out, but that was a small price to pay. We certainly had no intention of killing the girl, and if that surprises you, think about it a minute.

In the first place, I was no homicidal maniac and I assumed Ash wasn't, either. The Broker didn't take on people who took pleasure in killing; he took on people who could kill dispassionately, and well.

Furthermore, kill one guy and it's a killing; kill two or more and all of a sudden it's a mass murder. The papers and TV start hollering psychopath on the loose, or in this instance splashing "Love Nest Slaying" all over the place, and pretty soon an unnatural interest has been stirred up in what otherwise would have been considered a routine occurrence, buried in the back pages of the papers, unworthy of more than a mention on the tube.

So when I was hired, as part of a team, to kill somebody, that one somebody got it, and nobody else. Period. Anything else is just plain bad business.

If I thought life was cheap, I wouldn't charge so much to take one.

Anyway, the stakeout had been uneventful. Working backup is always boring, and for that reason I avoided it whenever possible; but this guy was especially boring. A goddamn robot. No variety whatsoever, every day the same clockwork run-through.

But thank God for Tuesday and Thursday, and those long lunches at the Tuck-a-Way Motel. Seeing him duck into that motel room, a few minutes after that cheap little blonde had done the same, and catching a glimpse of an awkward but impassioned embrace, made him seem almost human.

We took a week and a half, a full week of stakeout, just me alone, checking out what we'd been told about the mark's habit pattern, and another half a week with Ash, joining me on stakeout, even spelling me one evening so I could catch a movie and relax a little, and just generally getting filled in from me on the mark's pattern and the overall lay of the land.

Came Thursday of that second week, an uncharacteristically cool and overcast day for the middle of July in the Southwest, and we were ready to go. I'd taken a room directly opposite theirs (or as directly opposite as possible, considering the motel was L-shape) and from the window we watched the two bodyguards deposit the mark at the door of the room, saw a flash of blond hair as the couple embraced, watched the two bodyguards exchange weary grins, shake their heads, and walk across the street to the greasy spoon, leaving their car behind in a stall by the room.

We waited five minutes, and Ash took off. He was going in through that back window, which we'd already broken the lock on this morning, having been in the motel room for a look around and to prepare. We'd considered having Ash simply wait inside, just hide in the room, but we figured there was always the outside chance the bodyguards would step inside and check the room over first. They hadn't ever done that, but we couldn't be sure. The stakeout had lasted only a week and a half, and I'd witnessed the ritual at the Tuck-a-Way a mere three times.

I have no idea why the bodyguards came back. They didn't come back in a hurry, so they apparently hadn't got wind of what we were up to. They could hardly have received a phone message for their boss over at the greasy spoon, unless they were in the habit of letting it be known they could be reached there Tuesday and Thursday afternoons, which was possible, I guessed. The nearest I could figure was the mark had forgotten to take his heart medicine (did I mention he had a bad heart?) but that's just a guess.

At any rate, as I watched from the window, I suddenly realized the two guys who had strolled calmly into my line of vision were heading for the door of the same room I was watching, and shit! Fuck, if it wasn't the fucking body-guards!

Somehow I got there at the same time they did. I don't really remember how. I ran, but had the presence of mind not to wave my gun around as I did; I was carrying it under a folded raincoat, which I had over my arm, and I didn't even drop the raincoat as I sprinted across the motel court and went through that motel room door right as they were opening it, right behind them, knocking both of them to the floor, kicking the door shut behind me, slapping first one, then the other on the back of the head with my auto-matic, then slapping each of them on the back of the head again, to make sure they were out, and when I looked up I saw Ash standing there, smoke coming out of his silenced nine-millimeter, the mark sitting up in bed, naked, top of his head gone, toupee and all, the girl in a naked, uncon-scious lump on the floor by the bed, and Ash said, "Jesus, Quarry. I guess I owe you one."

I said I guessed he did, and suggested we get the fuck out of there.

But that was four years ago, and people have a way of forgetting. And if Ash hadn't forgotten, he had a funny way of paying me back, sending people round to kill me and all.

Anyway, the situation had changed somewhat.

Now I owed him one.

8

I looked up and saw Ash.

It was midafternoon, and I was in a phone booth. The booth was in the lobby of the Holiday Inn that had sent "Raymond Drake" a room confirmation. The Holiday Inn was on the outskirts of Davenport, Iowa, which is part of the Quad Cities, a half-million-plus metropolitan area straddling the Mississippi River; last time I was here I'd been on the Illinois side, at a Howard Johnson's in Rock Island, meeting the Broker.

I was calling Ash's room to see if he was in or not. And if not, planned to go find a maid to bribe, so I could get in the room and poke around. While I was sitting there letting it ring, he walked right by me.

He didn't see me. He was walking toward the coffee shop, glancing at a newspaper, and he didn't see me.

I slid out of the booth, wandered over to the check-in desk, and leafed absently through free-take-one brochures detailing fun things to do in the Cities. Ash was hanging his overcoat on a rack just inside the coffee shop. The doors were spread open and I could see him clearly. He took a stool at the counter, ordered from the menu, returned to reading his paper.

Something was different about him. What was it? He

was wearing a more expensive-looking suit than he used to, and that fur-trimmed brown leather overcoat alone must've cost an arm and a leg, or at least an arm. But that wasn't it, nor was it the slight gut he'd put on that on anybody but a slender type like him would be nothing.

It was the hair.

His curly red hair. He'd had it straightened. And styled, covering up his little bald spot. Ash had come up in the world, it seemed, and it had gone to his head. Straight to his head.

Having the overcoat with him meant one of two things: either he was on his way out, and stopping off at the coffee shop for something before he left; or he was just getting back from somewhere, and stopping off at the coffee shop for something before going back to his room.

Either way, his room would be empty for a while.

So I went into the coffee shop myself, head lowered, scratching my forehead, keeping my face obscured. I went straight to the coatrack. It was not a busy time of day, and the nearby register was, for the moment, unattended. Ash was drinking coffee, reading the paper; his back was to me.

I pretended to be looking above the coats, where hats were stowed, as if I'd lost something, keeping a low but aboveboard profile as my left hand dug into the right-hand pocket of Ash's expensive overcoat, from which I took his room key, gave up my search for the imaginary item I'd lost among the hats, and left.

I did glance back, well out into the lobby, but Ash hadn't

noticed me, and neither had any of the coffee shop help, apparently.

I'm not going to waste time describing what Ash's room looked like. If you've never seen a room in a Holiday Inn, you're either from another planet or lucky. I looked in the closet, found four suits hanging, all of the same well-tailored, costly nature as the one I'd seen him wearing. Also a raincoat, several pair of shoes, several empty suitcases. His shaving gear was in the john. I poked through the bureau drawers, found nothing. Nothing that told me anything special, that is: shirts, shoes, ties, underwear, box of ammo. The ammo was no great surprise. After all, I didn't figure he was here on vacation.

But then, I didn't figure he was here to kill anybody, either. He had sent others to do that, in my case; and he was now supposedly in the process of moving into the bloodless end of the killing business, into the role of assigning jobs, not carrying them out. Still, Ash was in the habit of carrying a gun, and why should he be expected to change? The Broker never carried one, but Ash wasn't the Broker; Ash had come up through the ranks. So the box of ammo was nothing special, probably. I covered it back up with some of his jockey shorts and closed the drawer.

I shook the room down pretty good, considering I didn't want to leave a mess. Went through the pockets of any piece of clothing that had pockets, got nowhere. Found a notepad by the phone, the top sheet of which had some doodles on, but nothing decipherable. I did find another sheet, crumpled up in the wastebasket by the desk; I unwadded it and for my trouble got "apt 6." In the john I dug through his shaving bag and found deodorant spray, toothpaste, toothbrush, shave cream, aftershave, an electric razor, and a bunch of other stuff that normally would've been unpacked by now. He'd been here overnight, and he wasn't packing to leave, so why was all this stuff stuffed in the shaving bag? Ash was not exactly compulsively neat, you know.

Under the false bottom I found two spare .45 barrels, a spare silencer, a can of 3-in-1 oil, cleaning tools, and rag.

A box of ammo was one thing; this was something else again.

When I got back to the coffee shop, Ash was just finishing a plate of something. I dropped his key back in his overcoat pocket, and went out in the lobby. I was looking at the free brochures again when Ash came out and headed for his room.

I'd had a good two minutes to spare.

9

It was cold, sitting in the car, and after a while I turned the engine on and got the heat going. I had no idea how long a wait I'd have. Possibly Ash would stay in his room the rest of the day, on into evening; if he was coordinating the activities of others, subordinates might be coming directly to his motel room for instructions and to make reports, in which case he might not be coming out of there for days, or even weeks.

Of course, he'd already been out once today, which seemed to discredit the notion of his working strictly out of the Holiday Inn; but since he hadn't been in town long, he might have gone out to set some things in motion, which only now enabled him to settle down in his room for a long winter's nap.

And then I stopped worrying about it. It was warm in the car now, and I was comfortable, and as long as Ash didn't stay in there forever, I was going to see him leave. The only way out of the parking lot, which separated the motel from the highway, was around front. And that's where I was parked, sitting, waiting.

Dusk set in and it got hard to see the faces in the cars pulling out of the lot. I had the Buick parked toward the middle, so I could keep track of both exits, one on either side; but I doubted Ash would be heading out of town, which is the way the exit on the left would take him, so when dusk began turning to dark I moved the car to a free stall next to the exit on the right, assuming when Ash left the motel he'd be heading toward the Cities. At the same time I tried to keep tabs on the cars that were turning out that left way, toward the Interstate, but that was damn near impossible. There were a few streetlights and some light from the motel itself, but that wasn't enough, and I soon gave up trying to monitor both exits, which is the reason why by midevening I was getting worried again, and bored and hungry, and I glanced at the driver in the car easing up alongside me, and it was Ash.

Again, he didn't spot me. He was behind the wheel of a Ford LTD, and was looking both ways, checking traffic, and pulled out and drove toward Davenport.

So did I.

I followed him down Brady Street, with its four lanes and constant flow of cars to cover me, followed him down into a neon and plastic canyon of franchise restaurants, auto dealerships, and discount stores, which briefly leveled off exits into an improbably sedate middle-class neighborhood that might well have been offended by having all this traffic running through the middle of it. The intersection up ahead gave off the glare of another commercial district, but before we got there, Brady became a one-way going the other way, and Ash and I and the other cars were guided by directional signs onto a side street that skirted a peaceful-looking, snow-covered park right off a Christmas card, and then around onto another major street, Harrison, a one-way running downhill toward the river, running downhill in more ways than one, cutting through another commercial area that soon degenerated into what might be charitably called a lower middle-class neighborhood, and this is where Ash turned off, taking a right, plunging into the city's unacknowledged black ghetto, a poorly lit, rundown area where sagging old double-story houses sat so close to each other the curls of peeling paint all but touched.

Up till now, there'd been plenty of traffic to hide behind, but not here. Ash was driving slow. The blocks were short, streets crisscrossing irregularly and often. It was a neighborhood you want to drive through quickly, but can't. Ash, in his new clothes and expensive car, was out of place, and so was I; I was bound to be spotted by him, before long. I laid back as much as possible, wondering what possessed Ash to cut through this part of town, and assumed he was on his way elsewhere, and then he pulled over.

Pulled over and parked, and I coasted by him moments later, face turned away, acting like a stranger lost and looking for a street address.

I figured he made me, made me a long time ago and sucked me in here and pulled over just to flush me out, and when I circled back around the block expected him to be long gone. He wasn't. He was just sitting there, motor running, parked. I turned off a side street, to avoid passing right by him again, and came around from the other direction, and pulled in along the curb a block up from him, behind an old Volkswagen, which provided some cover for me but didn't entirely block my view.

And so I sat. This time I didn't dare leave my motor on, so I had to sit in the cold. I wondered if this was a Mexican standoff of some kind. Wondered if Ash had in fact spotted me, perhaps even spotted me pulling in behind the Volks, and was waiting me out. If so, we might both have a long wait. I settled down in the seat, arms folded, hands tucked in my armpits to keep warm; in my right hand, of course, was the silenced nine-millimeter, providing its own sort of warmth.

I saw the kid immediately, rounding the corner just beyond the Volks I was parked behind. A white kid, long straight hair, full-face beard, old Navy surplus overcoat. Looked like a college kid, or perhaps college dropout or hanger-on. Hands in his pockets, strolling along, nice and easy. Maybe he was stoned; anyway, he moved that way.

Heading toward Ash's parked car.

The kid—if that's what he was—got in on the rider's side and soon I could see smoke curling and collecting in there, as he and Ash sat in the car smoking as they talked. And they talked a long time. A solid half-hour.

Superficially, it looked like a dope buy. Rundown neighborhood, guy in a fancy suit and fancy car, talking with hippie type. Making a connection. Anyone in this neighborhood who had witnessed what I had would probably assume that. And around here chances were nobody would think much of it, either.

But it went on far too long for a dope buy, and of course Ash wasn't into that...at least as far as I knew.

No, this was something else. Something I was beginning to recognize the pattern of.

And when the kid finally got out of the LTD and started strolling back the way he came, I let Ash go and picked up on the kid. On foot.

I walked on the other side of the street, a block back; I was still wearing the same clothes that allowed me to pass as a college kid myself, this morning. He didn't spot me. Or, if he did, he was good at pretending he didn't.

Within the space of a few short blocks, the tenement surroundings changed. The crowded-together two-story houses began disappearing, and in their place were grotesquely beautiful onetime mansions. Not that the change in appearance of the neighborhood was an entirely radical one; this, too, was a rundown area, and the Gothic old homes showed signs of decay, were even crumbling in some cases. Like the somewhat similar—if less elaborate—house in Milwaukee where Ash stayed, these homes all seemed to have been converted into apartment houses. Judging by the vans and compact cars in the parking lots carved out of the once well-kept and spacious lawns, I gathered that what had once been the homes of the city's elite now provided housing for college students from the several nearby campuses.

He entered one of the largest of those huge old homes,

a yellow, paint-peeling, clapboard palace with spired towers whose upper windows were stained glass. The place looked like it might hold a dozen or more efficiency apartments, and had a "Rooms for Rent" sign in one of the front windows. As I stood facing the house I could see three windows on the second floor that were dim, as the kid went in, and then after he'd had time to climb a flight of stairs, a light went on in one of those windows, and then went out again moments later. I checked my watch: it was a few minutes before nine. Ash's long-haired friend either went to bed very early, or was coming out of there again.

Ten minutes passed and no sign of him, through the front way, and I began wondering if he'd seen me and sneaked out a back door. I was leaned against a tree, gun still tucked under my arm, so I wasn't worried, and as I was studying from an angle the window of what I assumed to be his room, I saw something glint.

Something glass, catching light from a street lamp.

Across the way from the big yellow apartment house was another of those Gothic homes, a brown brick affair that was unique looking even among these once-distinguished neighbors. It was somewhat smaller than the others, and had been designed to look like a modern castle, with turrets and everything, and seemed well-maintained, with no lawn full of cars to indicate apartment house conversion.

Somebody living in that place was going to die. Probably soon, judging by the length of the conversation between Ash and the kid, who was sitting in his room by the window right now, using binoculars or perhaps a sniper scope to study the mark.

That "kid" was the backup man, and Ash was the trigger. Somebody in that brown brick castle was the target.

Now, where did *I* fit in?

10

The water in the pool was warm. Too warm, really. I prefer a pool where the water's on the chilly side. But of all the hotels and motels in Davenport, this place, the Concort Inn, was the only one with an indoor pool, so considering the time of year, if I wanted to swim, this was going to have to do.

And I wanted to swim. I swim every day, if I'm able. It keeps me in shape. Relaxes me. Helps me think, if I need to. Helps me not think, if I need that.

This morning I needed to think. Last night I'd been too tired to lose any sleep over the jumble of matters that needed sorting out, urgent matters though they were. I'd been up since this started, since night before yesterday when those two guys invaded my place in Wisconsin, so after my excursion last night into that neighborhood of crumbling mansions, I'd gone straight to the only place in town I knew of where I could find both bed and pool to dive into.

The Concort Inn was a modern-looking monolith of a building, made of glass and plastic and blue-tinged steel, sitting near the government bridge on the edge of Davenport, on a sort of concrete oasis, a full block's worth of parking protecting the place from the seedy warehouse district at its back and the four busy lanes of traffic running in front. The rooms at the Concort were nice size, clean, pleasantly furnished and, since the building sat at an angle, usually had a decent view of the river. Downstairs was maybe the best restaurant in town, and a lounge with no cover and plenty of entertainment. All of which was pretty impressive, I suppose, if you hadn't been there a thousand times before. I had.

The Concort was where the Broker and I would get together before jobs. Some kinds of business you just don't handle by phone or through the mail, and every hit I ever made began with words rolling off Broker's politician-smooth tongue, in a room at the Concort. Every assignment of my five and a half years in the business I had picked up here, or practically all of them; a few had been at other motels or hotels in the area, but most had been right here. At the Concort.

Maybe I was an idiot, coming back here, staying here again. Maybe I was risking my ass, just so I could go swimming, for Christsake. Broker had money in the Concort, no question, and he used the hotel as a tool in his operation; and it might be logical to assume Broker's replacement would do the same.

Point of interest: Ash was operating not out of the Concort, but from the Holiday Inn near the Interstate.

Second point of interest: Ash and backup man were engaged in what looked to be a pretty much routine sort of hit.

And what that seemed to add up to was Ash was not the

Broker's replacement, but a hired hand, somebody else's flunky, only who was that somebody else? And why did that somebody else contract my death? Was there some sort of a power play going on here that I was caught in the middle of, several candidates going after Broker's job, preparing to engage in a shooting war, what?

Questions. Questions.

I floated on the water's warm surface, floated on my back, listening to the lapping sounds of the water, staring at the aqua-color ceiling, looking for answers.

"Oh...excuse me."

The voice came from behind me: feminine, soft, so soft it didn't even echo in a room that threw sound around so thoroughly the barest ripple of the pool caused a tremor.

I rolled off my back, snaked over to the edge of the pool before she was gone.

She'd come into the room, which was an aqua-blue cement box hardly big enough to hold the medium-size pool, and had apparently slipped off her robe before noticing me, and then when she did notice me was for some reason frightened, and said excuse me and was now getting back into her full-length white terry robe, heading toward the door.

"Hey!" I called.

My voice echoed like a yell off Lover's Leap, and it stopped her.

"What's to be excused?" I said, leaning against the edge of the pool.

She turned. Smiled a little. A good-looking woman of

maybe twenty-eight, with white blond hair that hung to her shoulders and the sort of face you see on the covers of classy fashion magazines.

"I just didn't know anyone was in here," she said, hugging her white robe to herself protectively.

"Well, I'm in here," I said, "and so what? This isn't exactly my private property, this pool. And I'm not going to bother you. So swim if you want."

She hesitated. Looked at me. Appraised me. "You don't mind...?" she asked.

"No."

She made a shy, shrugging gesture, let the terry robe fall in a puddle at her feet and dove in the pool. She swam easily, gracefully, though there was nothing fancy about it; she just swam, like she was born knowing how, neither gliding nor chopping: swimming.

I had my elbow on the edge of the pool, leaning there, watching her. After a while she swam over and sat up on the poolside, not particularly close to me, but close enough to talk without shouting. She sat there catching her breath, and I just kept looking at her. She had a nice body, and she made me wish I had the time to do something about it. She was slender, but not skinny, and she had the best-looking legs I'd seen in a long time. She wasn't really busty, but she had enough, and I was enjoying the way her nipples were pushing out at the thin nylon fabric of her simple one-piece black swimsuit.

I stayed down in the water, because something was pushing at the nylon of my swimsuit, too.

"They keep this pool too warm," she said, suddenly.

I said I agreed.

"I like to dive into cold water," she said. "Wakes you up. Slaps you around, a little. Gets your nerve endings working. Reminds you you're alive."

I said I couldn't agree more.

"You, uh...must think I'm pretty silly," she said.

"Why's that?"

"The, you know...fuss I made, when I came in."

"What fuss? You just didn't see me, and then you did, and it startled you. That's all."

"That's close, anyway," she said, smiling less tentatively now. "You see, I come in here every morning about this time, that is every weekday morning...what day is this?"

"Thursday."

"Thought I lost track for a minute. See, on the weekdays, around this time of morning, this time of year, pool's usually empty. I can have it to myself."

"Do you live here or something?"

"No. This hotel, you mean? No. I'm local, live here in Davenport. The manager is a friend. He lets me swim here when I want."

"You do that often, do you? Swim here?"

"Lately, I have. I've...I've been going through a kind of a rough period, personally, and I don't get out much. Coming here during the week, in the middle of the morning, that's about it for me, lately. I've got a lot on my mind, and coming here, swimming here, alone, seems to help me get myself together, a little."

"I can understand that."

"Really?"

"Sure. I'm a junkie where swimming's concerned. Don't miss a day, if I can help it."

"No kidding?"

"No kidding. And I suppose for much the same reasons as you. I even agree with you about swimming alone. I try to find a pool where I can do some nice solitary swimming, myself, when I can."

"Well," she said. Very pretty smile. Blue eyes, that light, clear blue. "I guess I've found a kindred spirit."

"I guess so."

"My name's Carrie."

She seemed to want a name from me, so I gave her one.

"Mine's Jack," I said.

"How long are you going to be in town, Jack?"

"I'm not sure. A week, maybe."

"Then maybe I'll see you here tomorrow," she said, and got up, got her robe, and was gone.

I sat staring at the door for a good solid minute.

Then I swam some more.

11

Ash's big shiny new LTD was sitting in the lot at the Holiday Inn, just as I expected it to be. And Ash would be in his room. Staying put. Not straying from his phone, in case his backup man should need to reach him.

And I was in my big mud-spattered used Buick, parked in the front lot of the motel, watching. I didn't figure Ash to come out of there till evening, but I sat and watched just the same. When you're working on supposition, as I was, you account for every possibility.

Even so, I was a little lax about getting started, and my vigil didn't get under way till around noon. I'd had a good breakfast at the Concort, before my midmorning swim, and on my way out I spent ten minutes in the lobby at the newsstand, finally settling on a couple of paperback westerns and *Penthouse* magazine, anticipating a long, boring afternoon at the Holiday Inn.

And then I'd gone back to that neighborhood of decomposing dreams, driving around for half an hour through those several Gothic blocks, to get a look at things in the light of day (albeit a cloudy one). Most of those big old houses looked worse, paint chipping and peeling like a cheap whore's layered makeup; almost none of them looked better, with a notable exception being that brown brick structure, which even in the better light showed no signs of decay. It sat, aloof, with a huge snow-covered lawn separating it from the lawn-turned-parking-lot of the peeling yellow monster next door, where Ash's backup man was playing college-boy boarder. It was the last house on the block, perched on the edge of an impossibly steep hill, the street dropping sharply to intersect another half a block below. The landscape between was thick with skinny trees whose gnarled, twining branches reached out at odd angles, hovering over patches of snow, patches of dead grass, patches of bare earth that looked like some strange disease of the scalp. Perhaps if it hadn't been winter, this tangle of branches and lumpy earth might have been pleasant to look at. As it was, it was dead and ugly and a disturbing contrast to the modern-day castle overlooking it.

The most important thing about that weird stretch of landscape was it made an approach from the rear of that brown brick palace almost impossible. The front of the house faced the lawn and that big yellow dump across the way, with the street on the one side, and more lawn on the other. So, if I was right, and Ash was planning to go in there and kill somebody in that place, he was going to be pretty conspicuous going in. Unless he planned to play *Guns of Navarone* and scale that steep, briar-patch of a hill to go in the back way, which was pretty conspicuous itself, considering doing that he'd be in full view of all four lanes of Harrison Street traffic.

I thought about all of that, as I sat in the Buick in the Holiday Inn lot, between leafing through the *Penthouse* and reading one of the paperback westerns. And soon the afternoon slid uneventfully into evening.

Or, almost uneventfully.

Around four-thirty someone interesting entered the motel. Forty-five minutes later, give or take a minute, he came back out again.

His name was Curtis Brooks, and he was a lawyer, a trial lawyer. I had never met the man, but I knew of him. So would you, if I was using his right name. He was the most widely publicized, nationally known resident of the Quad Cities, except for maybe that lady mayor in Davenport, who temporarily eclipsed him.

Basically, what he did was see to it guilty people were found innocent.

He walked right by me, on his way to his Lincoln Continental, leather overcoat slung absently over his arm, as if he'd forgotten it was cold out. He was alone. He looked worried. Somebody in the parking lot recognized him and spoke, some businessman, and Brooks put on a smile and waved to the man, and then looked worried again.

He was smaller than I imagined. A handsome man with a Florida tan and character crinkles in all the right nooks and crannies of his face, wavy brown hair with solid white around his ears, large, intense, expressive brown eyes, expensive suit. Very expensive suit, such as to put the come-up-in-the-world Ash down.

Speaking of Ash, there was no reason, really, to connect Brooks to him. Brooks was a man whose reputation was colorful, but whose criminal connections were strictly lawyer/client. At least that's what his p.r. man would tell you.

I knew the odds were good Brooks had just been to see Ash. There was a logical common bond between the two men. Both of them were in the murder business, Ash carrying them out, Brooks covering them up. Also, it seemed more than likely that Brooks, of all the lawyers in the Quad Cities, would have been the Broker's. Especially considering how often the lawyer had represented the courtroom interests of various elements of organized crime.

What I didn't know was the subject matter of the conversation between Brooks and Ash. The takeover of Broker's operation? That brown brick castle hit? Both? Neither? What?

And so I sat in the Buick in the Holiday Inn parking lot, thinking about those and other things, and at seven-twenty Ash drove out of the lot and I followed him.

12

It was the same routine as the time before. Ash drove into the ghetto neighborhood, pulled up along the curb, and waited. A few minutes later, his long-haired associate came strolling onto the scene, from the direction of that yellow former mansion. I was parked up a good three blocks from them, where it wasn't likely I'd been seen, but I didn't plan to stick around, anyway. Why should I sit and watch them talk? I had something better to do.

After all, you can work on supposition only so long. There comes a point where you have to match up all that supposing with what's really going on.

So, while the two conspirators sat conspiring in the LTD, I drove a few blocks, parked across from a certain seedy-looking yellow apartment house, walked over, and went in the front door.

There was a vestibule, with a grid of cubbyhole mailboxes nailed to either wall, and beyond that a hallway to the left, a wall with a few doors to the right, and in front of me directly was a stairway, going up to that second floor where Ash's backup man had a room. Of course, that part was supposition: his being Ash's backup man. And that was why I'd come here, to poke around the guy's room while he and Ash were busy talking in that fancy-ass Ford a couple blocks over.

The place was pretty rundown. Both floors displayed faded, curling, ugly-to-begin-with wallpaper, and throw rugs that were as frayed as they were colorless, with good solid wood floors showing around the edges of the rugs, floors which unfortunately hadn't been varnished for decades. There had been *some* remodeling done, how-ever: a cheap, sloppy job of remodeling that neither the people who hired it done nor the people who did it could feel any pride about, as evidenced by the modern-style light-color plywood doors stuck in the middle of walls otherwise trimmed with dark, rich, occasionally carved woodwork dating back to the turn of the century, easy.

The numbers on the doors were black numerals on a cheap glitter-gold background, those stick-on things you can buy at a hardware store to put on an outdoor mailbox. I was trying to figure out which room was the one I was after, remembering the approximate position of the window where I'd seen the guy doing apparent stakeout duty; I passed numbers 4 and 5, and when I came to 6 remembered that scrap of paper in Ash's motel room that had said "apt 6" on it, and smiled.

I looked around. The hallway was empty. I could hear rock music, seeping out from under the door across from me. I could smell various cooking smells, mingled to-gether. People were around, but none of them were in the hallway, at the moment.

I put my ear to the door, in case number 6 somehow

turned out to be somebody else's room after all, and just to see if anybody was in there, a shack-up girl maybe… though if this was a stakeout point (as I was almost sure it was) no one else would be in there. Not a girl, not anybody. It's not the kind of job you take your wife or lover along on, and you even stay away from pickups and whores. If you get horny, you just whack off, and that's all there is to it.

I used a credit card to unlock the door. I have a dozen keys on a ring that I always carry with me, and between them, those keys will open about any door outside of a bank vault. But I rarely have to use those keys. The typical apartment door these days is the type that you can open with a credit card, and in the Midwest, which hasn't as yet got as paranoid as elsewhere (with the possible exception of Chicago and a few other of the larger cities), you don't often run into doors with night latches and/or other safety lock sort of features.

Did I mention I was wearing the college kid getup, again? Well, I was. Did I mention I had the nine-millimeter in my right hand, with my raincoat slung over my arm to cover the gun? Well, I did.

With the door unlocked, I stepped to one side, nudged it open with my foot, and waited for something to happen. When nothing did, I went in. Low. Cutting to the left, getting a quick look around the room from the admittedly dim light of the hallway, before shutting the door with my heel.

I stood there in the darkness for a couple minutes, not

breathing, listening to see if anybody else was. When I was convinced I was alone in there, I found the light switch on the wall behind me, flicked it on, and dropped to the floor.

When still nothing happened, and seeing no one in the room, I did one final precautionary number with the closets (there were two), and finding them empty (of people), got to work.

I didn't have much to do. Ash's backup man had done it for me. And he *was* Ash's backup man, no doubt about that. An easy chair had been pulled around by the window, and binoculars were on the sill. On the arm of the nearby couch was a notebook, recording activities of the subject in the brown brick castle across the way. There was no name, of course, just a time chart of "Subject's Movements." I couldn't risk giving the chart more than the most cursory of examinations, but it didn't take much of one to see that this particular subject wasn't going to make the toughest target in the world, considering said subject lived alone and seemed to stay home constantly.

I glanced through the binoculars, over toward the brown brick place. I studied all the windows, but saw no one; all drapes were drawn. I looked over at the garage, which was a separate little brown brick building near the house, and saw the double door go up, suddenly, thanks to some automatic device, I guessed, and a car drove out, a Pontiac Grand Prix. The garage door shut itself, and the Grand Prix pulled out into the street and was gone.

I hadn't got a look at the driver, but whoever it was,

this marked a significant departure from the backup man's time chart, a departure that would go unrecorded, and I took some mild pleasure in knowing that Ash and his pal had unwittingly screwed up. Since the record didn't show any visitors tonight—and, judging by my quick flip through the notebook, there had never been any visitors since the stakeout began, either—I could safely assume the person who had driven off in that Grand Prix was the mark. Meaning a screwup serious enough to cost Ash and his pal an extra week of work, maybe, till they were again sure they had the mark's schedule down pat.

I didn't want to hang around too long, of course, so I began giving the rest of the one-room efficiency apartment a quick once-over. There was the usual secondhand furniture, more faded wallpaper, more frayed throw rugs, a kitchenette over in the corner, and the couch that would open out into a bed. In the chest of drawers I expected to find a box of slugs or, anyway, something of that sort among the guy's clothes.

Only there weren't any clothes in the chest of drawers.

But there was a suitcase, I finally noticed, over by the wall. Packed and ready to go.

Which meant one thing, and one thing only: *Tonight*, as the saying goes, *was the night*.

The backup man would be coming back here, soon probably, to sit at the window and watch the brown brick house while Ash went in and did his thing. After which both of them would split.

Which was what I had to do, and fast.

I took a quick look around to make sure I hadn't left any signs of my poking around, and got out of there, holding onto that nine-millimeter like a mother holding onto a kid. Or, maybe it was the other way around. I locked the door behind me as I left, and on the stairs I bumped into him.

The backup man.

I said excuse me and went on.

He said, "Hey…"

I turned around. Smiled.

I hadn't seen the guy up close before. As I'd expected, he didn't look quite so young, up close. He was on the short side, but wide in the shoulders and probably a strong son of a bitch. The long straight hair and full face beard gave him the desired hippie effect, but the cold little eyes said Vietnam. I hoped he wouldn't see the same thing in my eyes. One item in my favor: his hands were exposed, and had nothing in them. He didn't seem to realize how close he was to dying right now, closer to dying than a guy in a VW on a mountain road with two semis coming straight at him. Which is to say, he didn't seem to realize what was under the raincoat slung over my arm.

He said, "I haven't seen you around here before."

I said, "I never been here before."

He said, "Why not?"

I said, "Because it's the first time I got the bitch to fuck me in a bed instead of in my fucking back seat, if it's any of your fucking business, you nosy asshole."

He studied me a second.

And then grinned.

"Sorry, man," he said. "We had some guys rip us off here last week. Just checkin' you out."

I shrugged. "Forget it."

We both waited a second for the other to leave, and finally he went on up the stairs, keeping an eye over his shoulder at me as he went, but smiling, waving a little as he disappeared from view.

I went on down, not looking back, wanting to, but not doing it. If he was up there, looking down at me, like I knew he would be, I couldn't afford to be looking back. That could be enough to confirm suspicions he might have. And I could feel his eyes on my back, and my hand tightened around the gun and Jesus I wanted to look back, but I didn't.

And then I was in the Buick again, starting it up, driving out of that goddamn neighborhood, and I noticed Ash, on foot, on the sidewalk, on his way to that brown brick palace with a gun in his pocket.

Which struck me funny, since nobody was home.

13

"I almost gave up on you," she said.

She startled me. I didn't know anyone else was in there. I'd come in, glanced around the room, seeing nothing but the pool and the aqua walls and the shadowy reflecting of the water on the walls, no one sitting around poolside, no sign of motion in the pool itself, and got out of the robe and folded it and put both robe and towel-wrapped gun on the floor, ready to dive in, when she spoke.

Those light-blue eyes of hers were peeking up over the edge of the pool at me, from just a few feet away. Her white-blond hair was wet and flat against her head. It made her look young.

I sat down next to the robe and towel and smiled. "I didn't expect to see you till tomorrow morning."

"I didn't expect that, either."

"What happened?"

"I got the urge to swim."

"I see."

"Sometimes you just get the urge, you know."

"I know. I like to, a couple times a day, if I can."

"Like to what?"

"Swim."

The lighting in the room, over the pool especially, was

subdued. On either end of the pool was some space for deck chairs, above which were windows in the ceiling (the pool room was on the top floor of the Concort) that during the day let in natural light, and in the summer were opened for purposes of suntanning. But it was winter now, and nighttime as well, and there wasn't any sun coming in those ceiling windows. And, as I said, the lighting over the pool itself was subdued.

"We seem to have the room to ourselves again," she said.

"We seem to."

"You want to come in for a swim, or you just going to sit there?"

"Come up here a minute."

"No, you come on in."

"Please."

"Well...all right."

She pushed up out of the pool and emerged shyly, per-haps embarrassed about the brief two-piece suit she had chosen to wear, a white suit clinging wetly to her, in place of the black one-piece she had worn this morning.

"Come here a second," I said.

"I'll get you wet," she said, grinning, dripping.

"Bend down."

She bent down.

I gave her a nice, soft hello kiss, a little kiss, and then drew back and waited.

She took my hand and tugged and I got to my feet, and she pressed herself to me and gave me an altogether dif-ferent sort of a kiss.

"You got me wet," I said.

"I warned you."

"How did you know I'd come swimming this evening? How long were you prepared to wait for me?"

"I didn't know, and who says I was waiting for you? Not longer than midnight."

Then she pushed away from me playfully and dove into the pool. She splashed around in there like a porpoise, and called at me to come on in, taunted me, and I said just a minute and walked over and looked out the door. The hall was empty. It was midevening, and the pool was open for use by Concort guests, but in the middle of winter, middle of the week, I didn't figure it would be too busy. So maybe nobody would notice and make a stink if I closed the door and flipped the lock.

I did that, and dove in after her.

We swam around and played like kids, splashing, chasing, dunking each other, all of that, in a good twenty-minute romp. Then she paddled over to the side and hugged it, hollering, "Base! Enough! Time out." She was out of breath, gasping for breath, and yet laughing at the same time. I paddled over to her.

"You…" she said, still trying to catch her wind, "…you locked the door."

"Just noticed that, did you?"

"Why'd you do that? Lock the door."

"I thought maybe we could use some privacy."

"What if somebody complains?"

"I'm a friend of a friend of the manager."

"Me, you mean."

"You."

"Well, I suppose that's right. Still…"

"Why, you got something against privacy?"

"No…"

"We talked about that this morning, remember?"

"What?"

"How nice it is swimming alone."

"Alone? There's two of us."

"Who's counting?"

"Who's swimming?"

Not us. I was holding onto her. I was up against her. She was holding onto the side of the pool with one hand and me with the other.

"Not us," I admitted. "Do you mind?"

"No."

"Have you ever done it in the water?"

"Done what? No."

"Me neither."

"Why…why do you ask?"

"I was just wondering what it would be like."

"I, uh…wonder."

My hand was cupping her ass now.

"I don't suppose anyone's ever done it in here," I said.

"I don't suppose. You think it's, uh, possible, here? I mean, this is the deep end."

"I wonder."

"But, uh…we'll never know, if we don't try, will we?"

"No," I said, slipping casually out of my trunks, "I guess not."

"And the door *is* locked…"

"Yes," I said, thumbs in the brief bottoms of her bikini, "it is."

And they slid right off her.

And I slid right into her.

Fucking in the water is a lot like drowning, I suppose, only when you go down for the third time, you don't give a damn. It's very noisy, at least the way we did it, thrashing around, clinging to each other or anyway me clinging to her while she hugged me with her thighs, pumping, churning, while trying to hold onto the edge of the pool behind her, but toward the end there she lost hold and we drifted away, locked together, and we were underwater, and we came under there, both of us, and we kicked to the surface and let loose of each other but stayed close, and gulped the air, and when we could, laughed, and then silently stroked over to the side of the pool. The whole thing lasted about three minutes, but they were three of the most enjoyable minutes I ever spent.

This time, I was holding onto the side of the pool, and she touched my shoulder and said, "Thank you."

"Are you kidding?"

"Not at all. You'll never know."

"Maybe I'd like to."

"Why…why don't we just, uh…leave it at thank you."

"Up to you."

"And I want you to know there's no obligation. You don't have to see me again, while you're in town, Jack.

Understand? If you don't want me to come here to swim tomorrow morning, or if you just don't want to show up yourself or something, fine, fine."

"You know what?"

"What?"

"It's hard to take a speech like that seriously, coming from somebody who doesn't have any pants on."

She looked down into the water, where her silky white-blond pubic hair was waving like provocative sea-weed, and she laughed again. "I see what you mean," she said, and touched me.

"You know something else?" I said.

"What?"

"I haven't eaten yet."

"In the water, you mean?"

I splashed her. "Supper."

"Oh. Neither have I."

"Want some? I hear there's a good restaurant down-stairs."

"Oh…I can't."

"Well. Up to you."

"No, it's not that…I just can't go down there, my hair, all wet."

"We could always go up to my room and call room service."

"We could do that."

We did.

First, I had to go deep-diving to retrieve my trunks and her bikini bottoms from the bottom of the pool, where they'd sunk like soggy stones; and then she got her robe, which she'd folded up and laid behind a deck chair, and stopped across the hall at the ladies' dressing room for her clothes, but went down in the elevator wearing her robe over her swimsuit, like I did.

When we got to the room, I called room service and was told it was too late for anything but drinks. She got on the phone and told them her name and they took her order: Chateaubriand for two and a bottle of red wine, which had an elaborate name and a date and all, and to someone like me who knows little or nothing about such things, that's pretty impressive. So was the service she was getting, at the drop of her name.

We turned on the TV and crawled onto the bed and fooled around awhile, and just when it was getting interesting, supper came. The nine-millimeter was still wrapped in the towel, and I stuck it under my arm as I answered the door, but supper was all it was, so I tipped the guy five and he went away and we ate. We didn't talk much at all, except to comment now and then on the television show we were pretending to watch. I did learn that she was a widow, a fairly recent one, and that this was a coming-out party of sorts for her.

I'd had a tingle about her all night, and not just sexual. She was real. She was not some whore sent around to set me up. In the first place, nobody knew I was in town, that I knew of, so nobody was likely to be setting me up. In the second place, the action she got on the phone, getting that after-hours room service, proved she was important in a way even the fanciest hooker can never hope to be. And that fast fuck in the pool had been real. Some sort of emotional purging for her. She was real. Nobody could be that good an actress.

But I had this goddamn tingle about her, and after she fell asleep, after we'd screwed a few times, I went through her purse, and found a picture in her wallet, a picture that I knew was of her late husband, knew it in my head and my gut simultaneously.

The picture was of someone I knew. Used to know.

The woman in my bed was the Broker's widow.

14

She was gone when I woke up.

For one groggy moment, I wondered where she'd gone, then remembered I'd heard her leaving, last night, around midnight. She'd got up, got her clothes on, got her things together, stopping momentarily to brush my face with her lips before she left. She was barely out of there when I was sitting up in bed, in the dark, pointing the nine-millimeter at the door. But the door didn't do anything, so after a few minutes I got out of bed, fastened the night latch, laid the gun on the nightstand, and slept through till nine the next morning.

This morning.

On the bureau I found a note she'd left, saying, "Think I'll pass on the morning swim. Call me this afternoon, if you want another evening one." Knowing her, that ambiguous use of the word "one" was on purpose. The note was signed, "Carrie," with phone number beneath.

I decided to pass on the morning swim, myself, and not just because she wasn't going to be there. Until now, I'd been reasonably convinced no one knew I was in town; but I couldn't be so sure, now that my easy poolside pickup of the evening before had turned out to be Broker's widow. I mean, I could hardly afford to just shrug and say, "Oh, so *that's* who she is. Isn't that an interesting coincidence." Not that coincidences don't happen, but in my position, chalking things up casually to coincidence could coincidentally lead to things going suddenly black…perhaps at the same time water in a swimming pool was taking on a reddish tone.

Cold needles of water struck my face, and I let them, wanted the water cold, showering and waking up at the same time, still thinking about Carrie and who she was. And the more I did, the less this seemed like a coincidence, or, anyway, the less it seemed a wildly, suspiciously improbable one. After all, I used to meet the Broker at the Concort, and knew that he had money in the place; well, now his wife had inherited his interest, and was it so unusual for her to come around and make occasional use of the pool?

This was, keep in mind, a young woman who evidently had been a showpiece—you should excuse the expression—for a husband twice her age, a bright, probably well-educated girl from a wealthy, sheltered background, no doubt, who would likely know little or nothing about her late husband's illicit business activities. The fact that Broker died a violent death, which had led to a partial public surfacing of the dark side of his business life, could explain her extended period of mourning, which had apparently ended last night, in the pool, in bed.

I thought about all that, going down in the elevator, and by the time I'd had breakfast, had made my mind up about something.

So far, these several days I'd been in town, I'd kept a low profile, and that had its advantages; but it gets boring in the shadows, after a while, and I never did enjoy doing stakeout work. Besides, after my run-in with Broker's wife, I was feeling confused, even paranoid, and enough of that. Time to come out.

Time to go see an old friend and say hello.

Time to see Ash.

15

It was almost warm. People were going around without coats. Occasional patches of snow remained, but that was about all. The ground was soft, the streets were slushy, but it was a nice day, for a change.

Then the sun slid under a cloud, the wind got some of its bite back, and I spotted Curtis Brooks going in the Holiday Inn.

I was just getting out of the Buick and was on my way to see Ash, when I saw the lawyer going in ahead of me. I laid back. Yesterday I had seen Brooks coming out of the motel and assumed he'd been to see Ash, and now today I'd be able to confirm or dispel that assumption. Only I was already convinced Brooks had called on Ash yesterday, so this would just get in my way. I wanted to confront Ash, but not with company around. And I might eventually want to confront Brooks, but not both of them at once.

Shit.

Brooks, by the way, seemed about as happy to be here as I was to have him here. All I got was a glimpse of him, before he ducked inside the motel, but that was all I needed to see how irritated he was. He had the frustrated, defiant gait of a constipated man on his way to complain about an out-of-order toilet, and the pained expression of somebody who just found out where his tax money was going. His frown threatened to put a crack in that Florida tan of his, and when a guy spoke to him in the lobby, old Public Image-conscious Curtis Brooks didn't reply.

I followed him through the lobby, down a couple of halls, and saw him stop to knock at one of the rooms. I walked on by, rather quickly, not especially wanting Ash to see me when he opened the door to let Brooks in.

I heard Ash say, "Can I fix you a drink, Brooks?" in a tone as embarrassingly chummy as it was contrite, and the door closed before Brooks could answer, if he did answer at all.

So. Brooks was pissed off, and Ash was apologetic. What that added up to was interesting enough to make me take back my negative reaction to the lawyer showing up here today.

Obviously, Brooks was here because Ash and the back-up man had fucked up last night, and the man's irritation was, of course, directly related to that. Which not only connected Brooks to Ash and the backup man and a proposed hit, but seemed to suggest Brooks was higher on the chain of command than Ash, confirming once and for all Ash was not the new Broker, and at the same time supplying a replacement candidate: Curtis Brooks himself.

But then, as an attorney, Brooks was a professional go-between, so by no means was it safe to assume he was the one who had taken over for Broker. Perhaps it was more likely that he had simply stayed along for the ride when the control of the Broker's operation shifted to someone else.

I went back out to the parking lot, back to my old stand, sitting in the Buick watching and waiting, just one more time. When Brooks came out of there, I'd go in.

And an hour later, Brooks came out, and I started getting out of the Buick, and saw Ash following on the lawyer's heels. Brooks still seemed irritated, but somewhat cooled down. Ash seemed less than totally subservient, but was obviously still trying to placate the man. They spoke for a few minutes, or rather Ash spoke and Brooks somewhat patiently listened, and then they got in their separate cars and drove out of the lot.

I followed.

Both men headed toward downtown Davenport, and once there, at the bottom of the hill, they split up, Brooks driving off toward the left, Ash to the right. I stayed with Ash, followed him onto Third, a one-way that began commercial and dwindled into residential. Ash stopped in an area where commercial and residential were uncomfortably commingled, and went into a diner, whose neon glowed the words "Chop Suey House" even in the afternoon.

I pulled in behind his LTD, and watched through the smudged windows of the place as he found a booth in the back. Inside the front window, two Oriental men in damp white outfits with aprons as smudged as the windows worked short-order style behind the counter, at a stove where two black metal woks were steaming, while nearby griddle and French-frying setups sizzled and smoked.

I went in, and the heat from cooking in that confined boxcar of a little room was overwhelming. One of the Orientals behind the counter greeted me, but I had no idea what he was trying to say. I greeted him, and he seemed to have no idea what I was trying to say.

It was well after lunch hour, and there were only a few people in the place, which at peak could hold maybe twenty-five. Ash was sitting in his back booth, face buried in the menu. He had taken off the coat of his expensive suit, and his shirt was long-sleeved and pastel yellow and his tie was a stylish brown and blue pattern. Every hair on his head was in place, a sandy red tapestry woven to conceal his bald spot.

He hadn't seen me yet.

I sat down across from him and said, "Still go for that Chink shit, do you?"

He looked up and blinked and said, "Hello Quarry," and went back to his menu.

"That's some car you're driving," I said.

He put the menu down, smiled. He seemed a little worn out, probably a combination of fucking up last night, and just having had to go through some sort of song and dance for the lawyer. "It gulps the gas, though," he said. "Otherwise, you're right. Some car. You like it, Quarry?"

"The car? LTD's not my style. I like a sportier number."

"Like that little fuckin' Opel of yours, you mean."

"Like that. Only I traded it in."

"What you driving, now?"

"That Buick, parked behind you." I pointed a thumb at the greasy window next to us, through which the two cars could be made out, barely.

"That's the kind of car you're partial to driving on a job, Quarry. You on a job?"

"Not exactly."

"Hey, let me order for you. You don't know Chinese food like I do. This little dump's supposed to be the best Chinese joint in town. I checked around. So leave it to me."

And about then an Oriental woman, who managed to look attractive despite her greasy white outfit and sweating brow, and who was somewhere between twenty and forty in age, asked us what we wanted, and Ash told her.

"So," Ash said, when she was gone, "you're not dead, Quarry."

"Not that you'd notice."

"Ha! Well, I want you to know I had nothing to do with that."

"With what?"

"Those two guys who came around to try and whack you out."

"That gives me a warm feeling inside, knowing that."

"Come on. What was I supposed to do? Warn you?"

"That would have been nice."

"Fuck. Who you tryin' to kid? In this business, any-body's a potential victim. You. Me. Those gooks over there, cookin' their butts off. Anybody. And people like you and me, we do what the guy with the money says to do. Nothing more. Nothing less."

"But you knew in advance, they'd be coming around? Explain that."

"I was the one who set it up."

"You're sure as hell hard to get information out of."

"What, do you think I'd fuck around lying to you? I set it up. Somebody hired me to set it up, I mean."

"Who?"

"That, I can't tell you. You know that, Quarry."

"I guess I do."

"But, like I said, I had nothing to do with it. You know, nothing personal."

"I know."

"I knew you weren't dead, when Lynch and Beatty didn't call in, afterwards. I figured they were at the bottom of some lake up there. That was no surprise. But I sure didn't expect you to come around here."

"What did you expect?"

"I expected you'd take it on the lam, what else? Just get the fuck out, go bury your head in Canada or Mexico or something, take your money, and make a new life or something."

"What money?"

"The money you saved from all your jobs."

"I spent most of that."

"Well, then, the money you made off of killing the Broker."

"I didn't kill the Broker."

"Okay, you didn't kill him. Whatever you say."

"Somebody figures I did, though."

"Right. And if you didn't kill him, who did?"

"A punk kid named Carl."

"The Broker's bodyguard?"

"Yeah. He was trying to shoot me, and I put the Broker between me and him."

"Well, you did kill the Broker, then, in a way."

"In a way."

"Why was the Broker's bodyguard shooting at you?"

"I told the Broker I was quitting. He thought I was pulling something, and was going to have me put away. It didn't work out the way he had in mind."

"Hey, that's a good story. Maybe the guy that put the contract on you would even buy it. I don't think so, though."

"Would it be worth a try?"

"Why the fuck ask me? I'm just another employee."

"I heard you took over for Broker."

"You heard wrong."

Our food came. Sweet and sour shrimp.

"What'd I tell you?" Ash said, his mouth full.

"It's good food," I said.

"Look. I'll do this much for you. I'll pretend I didn't run into you. I'll just look the other way, while you leave."

"Can I finish my food first?"

"Fuck, yes."

"And then I just take all that money I made off killing the Broker, and go to Canada or Mexico."

"Wherever you want. It's your money."

"There isn't any money. But suppose there was. Suppose I killed Broker, and got money for it. Why should anybody care?"

"How the fuck should I know?"

"I want to talk to the man you're working for. "

"Why?"

"I want to find out exactly why he wants me dead. I want to explain what really happened with the Broker."

"Then what?"

"Who knows? If he's taking over, maybe I'll want my old job back."

"I don't know, Quarry."

"Ask him."

"I don't know."

"It'd be a good idea to ask him."

"What the fuck…you threatening me, Quarry? What kind of shit is that?"

"You didn't ask me yet when I got in town."

"When'd you get in town?"

"Couple days ago."

"Couple days ago. What you been doin', since you got in town?"

"Nothing. Looking at dirty pictures and playing with myself."

"You'll go blind."

"I'll cover one eye."

"What the fuck you tryin' to say, Quarry? What you been up to around here?"

"Nothing. Vacationing. You know. Sightseeing."

"Sightseeing? In the Quad fucking Cities?"

"Sure. I got this camera. I take pictures of the sights."

"What sort of sights?"

"Oh, like the river. Important buildings. Classic old

homes. Like that brown brick number, up on the hill. You know. That place that looks like some sort of castle or something."

"When do you want to talk to him?"

"Give me a number I can call."

He got out a pen and wrote a number on a napkin. "Call this afternoon. Before four."

"I'll call sometime before midnight."

"Whatever."

"I want to thank you for your help, old buddy."

"It's okay. After all, you saved my life once."

"It was nothing. Believe me."

"You think I should've warned you, huh? Fuck, Quarry, you better than anybody ought to know it's not that kind of business."

"How much does it cost you, to get your hair puffed up like that, Ash? Covers up that shiny spot terrific."

"Fuck you, man. I like my car, *and* my clothes…"

"And your hair."

"And my fuckin' hair, too. I'm doing okay, Quarry, and you shouldn't begrudge me."

The Oriental woman came with the check.

"Look," he said, "I realize I owe you, for that time out west. Maybe I can find some way to pay you back for that, in spite of everything."

I pushed the check over to him. "Just pay for lunch. That'll make us even."

I had him leave before I did, and didn't follow him.

I had somewhere more important to go.

16

He was still up there. Watching. The sun was out again, and would glint occasionally off the binoculars, and that's how I knew. He was up there, in that dingy little efficiency apartment, on the second floor of that decaying yellow woodpile that used to be a mansion, watching out the window, watching the brown brick house across the way.

I'd been here all afternoon, sitting in the Buick, parked along the street across from where the apartment house parking lot met the castle's lawn. I was still dressed casually, like a college kid, and the nine-millimeter was in my lap, with *Penthouse* over it. It was five-thirty, and it had been a boring afternoon, but I'd found out what I came to find out.

They were going through with it.

It was a job that should have been scrapped a couple times already, but they were going through with it.

Last night Ash seriously screwed up, going in to make the kill and finding an empty house. That alone was enough to consider shelving all plans, stepping aside to let some other team come in and handle it at a later date.

Then today, over a plate of sweet and sour shrimp, he'd learned from me I'd been in town a couple days and had been watching him and his backup man, and knew they were planning to hit somebody in that brown brick house, and had pretended even to have been taking pictures of 'em, as I went.

And still they were going through with it.

I'd allowed Ash all afternoon to get in touch with his backup, plenty of time to tell the bogus hippie to get the hell out, which was the only logical thing to do in the situation. But here it was five-thirty, and there the guy was, sitting at his window, with his binoculars, watching the brown brick house across the way.

They were going through with it.

In spite of screwing up last night.

In spite of me.

And that meant whoever lived in that brown brick castle over there was somebody pretty goddamn special. Special enough to make a professional like Ash take risks he would normally never think of taking.

Somebody who had something to do with the takeover of Broker's operation, maybe. Otherwise, what the hell was Ash doing behind a gun? Ash wasn't a hitman anymore. He was an organization man. Second in command. Setting jobs up, not carrying them out. Now that Ash was moving up the criminal corporate ladder, it would take some very special target to rate his attention.

I sat there wondering who lived in that brown brick castle, wishing I'd checked into it sooner, not having realized before the importance of the potential victim living in that house, wondering if it would do any good to take down the address and go over to the public library and check the city directory, where I could match a name to the address, but who was to say that name would mean anything to me?

I got an answer to my question almost immediately, and without going to any library.

Just after six the Pontiac Grand Prix pulled out from the garage on the other side of the brick house, and glided out of the driveway and into the street. The car skimmed right by me, but the driver didn't notice me.

I noticed the driver.

She was on her way to meet me for an evening swim, even though I hadn't got around to calling her.

17

She was in a phone booth, in the Concort lobby, when I caught up with her.

I knocked on the glass, she opened the door and gave me an embarrassed look, and said, "I was just trying your room…"

"Never mind that."

"…you must think I'm terrible, chasing you like this. If you'd wanted to see me, you'd have called. I had no right coming around here and…"

I grabbed her by the arm and squeezed. Hard.

"I said never mind that."

"Wh…what's wrong? You're hurting me."

"I'm sorry," I said, easing my grip but not letting go.

"What's this all about, Jack?"

"You really don't know, do you, Carrie?"

"Know what?"

"Listen. Later we can sort this out. Right now I want to get you out of here, okay?"

"Why."

"Because someone's going to try to kill you."

At first she smiled, at first she thought I was putting her on, but then she studied my expression and thought a minute, and it sobered her.

"Does this have anything to do," she said, "with my husband being killed?"

"Yes, it does…and unless you're in a real hurry to join him, why don't you come with me?"

"Jack, I…I really don't know who you are. I mean, I…please don't misunderstand…but you're just a man I slept with once. Hell, not even that. We just, well, I just got laid by you a couple times, and that's about all there is to it, between us. That's about all I know about you."

"That's all I know about you, too, Carrie."

"No. No, you know more. I don't want to go anywhere with you until you explain this to me so I can understand it, all of it. Don't try to force me. I have friends here at the hotel I can turn to, if necessary. Some of them within earshot."

"You only have one friend in this hotel, Carrie, and I'm it. That you can depend on, anyway…anybody else here, who you consider a friend, is a friend through your late husband, am I right? And his friends, well, they may not be."

She considered that for a while, then finally said, "I'll go with you to your room. We can talk there. You had me there alone before, and didn't do anything to me I didn't want done, so…that much I'm willing to do. Then we'll see where we go from there…"

I didn't like it, really, but on the other hand I needed to clear my things out of the room, anyway; I didn't want to be hanging around this hotel anymore, and while nothing I'd brought with me ought to be too terribly incriminating, you never can tell. So I said okay, and we got on an elevator and had it to ourselves, thankfully. I looked at her, and she seemed shaken, but certainly not unhinged. I wished I was just taking her up there to climb in the sack with her again; she really looked fine, in her clinging sweater and slacks outfit, the same light blue as her eyes. I put that out of my mind, and asked her if there was any place I could hide her out for a few days.

"Like what sort of place?" she said.

"Do you have some girlfriend who's out of town, and has a temporarily vacant apartment? Something like that?"

"Well. I think I have something better, if you're really serious about this."

"I'm nothing if not serious, Carrie,"

"It's a cottage. On the Mississippi."

"Secluded?"

"Very much so. There's a bridge out on the only road that leads to the place. We can get there by another road, but'll have to walk the last half-mile or so."

"That sounds all right. That sounds pretty good."

"The bridge's only been out a few weeks, and the cottage hasn't even been shut down for the winter yet. There's still lights, and water. No heat, though. The place isn't heated, except for an old wood-burning stove."

The elevator doors slid open and we were on my floor. We didn't speak as we walked toward the room, and as I was digging in my jacket pocket for the key, I heard some noises coming from behind the door.

I raised a finger to my lips, and took her by the arm and led her back to the waiting area by the elevators.

"Somebody's in there," she whispered.

"That's right," I said.

"What are you going to do?"

"Go in and see who it is."

"Is that…wise?"

"Wise? I don't suppose so."

"What do you want me to do?"

"Get back on the elevator, go down one floor, and wait. I'll join you as soon as I can."

"What if you don't?"

"What if I don't what?"

"Join me. What if you never show up."

I punched the down button.

"Then you're on your own," I said.

I put her on the elevator, and she gave me a look like a person descending into purgatory, as the doors eased shut.

I went back to the room, and could still hear rustling around in there. No particular effort was being made to be quiet, which was good: it meant that if this was an ambush of some kind, it was in the early stages; whoever it was was presently ransacking the room, and hadn't got around yet to lying in wait.

I went over the layout of the room in my mind. Directly beyond the door was a brief hall or entryway, and beyond that was the bed, jutting out from the left wall, a night-stand on either side, a cushioned wooden chair in the left corner. The right corner was taken up by the windows, with no furniture to block the Concort's guaranteed river view; and across from the foot of the bed was a portable color TV on a stand, and next to that a dresser with a mirror. That dresser would not be immediately in sight as I came in, because the bathroom would be to my right and the closet to my left, putting me in a short, cramped hallway that obscured my vision of anything to the right of the TV. Judging from the sounds coming from behind that door, my intruder was presently going through the dresser. But there could be more than one person in there, too, and of course somebody could be in the bathroom or going through the closet, or any number of combinations of possibilities, so I could end up with quite a surprise party on my hands, going in there.

The only marginally sane way to play it was to turn the surprise party around on my guests; in other words, go in fast and let everybody get a look at my gun before they did anything rash.

I was so fast I surprised myself. I turned the key in the lock, shoved open the door, and dove through the entry- way, onto the bed, rolled off on the floor, and banged against the wall and wooden chair, but didn't lose control.

But the guy going through the dresser did.

He was medium-size. He looked like a college kid, but he wasn't the backup man, and he wasn't a college kid, either. Like me, like the backup man, like everybody else wandering around town pretending to be young, he wasn't. He was wearing a University of Iowa sweatshirt and brown jeans and used hairspray to keep his longish hair in place, and he just generally had the look of an insurance man playing dress-up. Or, rather dress-down. He was lean, but it wasn't the leanness of, say, a junkie; it was the leanness of somebody in shape. And while he had very few lines in his face, it wasn't from lack of age; it was from lack of emotion. He had those same cold Vietnam eyes as the backup man, and looking at him, I said to myself, *This fucker's a pro*, and to this day I don't know why he went for it.

Maybe he didn't think I'd shoot. Maybe he didn't know who I was exactly, or had been told I'd probably kill him if I got him in a situation like this, so was grasping for a straw. Whatever the case, he grabbed for the gun tucked in his waistband, a big goddamn thing, a .45 with a silencer half the size of the gun itself, and he almost had it out when my nine-millimeter quietly lifted the top of his head off and splashed the stuff inside all over the dresser mirror behind him.

He slid down the front of the dresser, his back closing drawers he'd opened. Most of what had been in his head was sliding down the mirror, which wasn't broken, the slug having been deflected off into the ceiling. His mouth was open and his eyes were rolled up, as if he'd tried, in his last fraction of a moment, to see what was happening up there, to watch his skull fragment and see the blossom of red and the color of his brains.

I got up, crawled across the bed, and shut the door before anybody came by sightseeing. There had been little noise. My nine-millimeter had made its near-silent thudding sound, and the guy had bumped up against the dresser, dying, but other than that, nothing. He hadn't had time to cry out. And somehow I didn't think he would have even if he'd had the time.

I gave him a quick frisk. He had a billfold, with maybe ninety dollars in it, a driver's license issued to James Hoffman, phony probably. Pockets empty, except for some sugarless gum.

So I packed my things. It was a little messy, moving him to one side to empty the dresser, but that was no big problem. I took his .45 with me, but it was too bulky to stick in my waistband, not with the nine-millimeter already stuck down there, warm against my flesh from recent use. I wrapped the .45 in a towel and stuffed it under my arm. I only had one bag and a shaving kit to tote, so the towel-wrapped .45 was no extra burden, really, and I was beginning to think having an extra gun could come in handy, now that the shooting was starting.

I hung the "Do Not Disturb" sign on the door, and went after Carrie.

18

I found her one floor below, waiting. Like she was supposed to be. That was encouraging. It had, after all, been her suggestion that we go to the room. I found it not entirely impossible that she might have been setting me up, but the look of relief on her face at seeing me made me tend to feel otherwise. Despite the elements of coincidence in my meeting her, and her turning out to be the target of Ash's afflictions, she seemed to be for real.

Or the best goddamn actress I ever ran across.

"Who was in there?" she asked.

"False alarm," I said. "Just a maid."

"A maid? With the door shut? Where was her cleaning cart?"

"She was in there watching TV and smoking a cigarette. I chased her out, but I admit it threw a scare into me. We'll have to scratch your idea about using my room to talk. It's just too dangerous staying around here."

"I gathered you'd made that decision," she said, wryly, seeing I was packed to go. "I suppose we can go ahead to the cottage, if you want. If you promise to fill me in on the way there."

"I promise."

We took the elevator down to the lobby. I got a few

dirty looks from bellboys who saw me carrying my own bags, but I got over it. I walked her over to the front entrance, where a doorman was posted, and people were pulling up in cars, coming to dine at the hotel's restaurant; that and various other continual activity made it a safe place to leave her, for a short time.

"I'm going to go get the car," I told her. "Stay right here. Close to people. If anybody tries anything, scream."

"That's terrific advice."

"It's the best I can do."

"I'll just walk with you to the car."

"No. It's in the rear lot, and it's not at all well lit back there. Too good a place for somebody to try something."

"I must be pretty popular."

"You don't know how popular."

The Concort sat on an entire block of parking lot, none of it lighted adequately except in front. The Buick was well toward the back; it was early evening, but dark. I'd left my bag and shave kit with Carrie, but still had the towel-wrapped .45 under my arm, and I almost dropped it when the guy jumped out from between two cars and grabbed me, just as I was nearing the Buick.

He slammed me up against a car and shoved a gun in my side and shoved a hand in my jacket and jerked my nine-millimeter out of my waistband and held it against my throat with his left hand, while putting his own gun, a .22 Ruger automatic with silencer, back in his belt.

It was the backup man, of course.

He pushed me, hard, and stood away from me, his

teeth white and grinning in the midst of his matted beard.

"So you followed us here," I said.

"I followed you here," he said. His voice was high-pitched and ruined the effect. I hadn't noticed his voice was high-pitched the other day; or maybe it just climbed the scale when he was excited. He was excited now. But despite that, and the cold eyes and wild beard and all, he didn't seem very sinister to me. I was having a hard time taking him seriously, especially now that the nine-millimeter wasn't against my neck anymore.

"What now?" I said. "If you talked to Ash, you know about me. You know killing me's not a good idea."

"Killing you's a very good idea. You're the cocksucker I bumped into in the hall, last night, aren't you?"

"You bumped into me in the hall. I'm not much on sucking cocks, though."

I was waiting for him to notice the bundled towel under my arm, but I guess he already had; he evidently knew about my swimming with Carrie, and thought nothing of it.

Meanwhile, he was shoving me again, still giving me that nasty white grin.

"You're in my way, asshole," he was saying. "I don't like assholes getting in my way and fucking things up for me. I don't give a damn what Ash says. Get out of my way, or I'm putting a hole in you."

"Let me know when you get to the scary part, will you?"

His sarcastic grin disappeared into the denseness of

facial foliage, and he swung the nine-millimeter around to slap me with it, and I let the gun-in-towel fall into my hands and gave him a hole in his chest that he looked down at once, unbelievingly, before pitching forward toward me. I stepped aside and let him slump against the parked car behind me, and then he dropped to the pavement like a wet bag of laundry.

Some people drove by in a Cadillac, but didn't notice anything, and when the lights of the Cad disappeared around the corner of the building, I stooped down and took his Ruger and put the nine-millimeter in his hand. I put the .45 in his waistband. I wasn't pleased about being left with a .22 as my only firepower, but it was just too convenient to pass up: the dead guy in my room had been killed by the nine-millimeter, and the backup man got his from the dead guy's .45. So they were tied together in death, whether or not they'd been tied together in life—though I assumed they were—and since there was nothing about the nine-millimeter to tie it to me, except for the fingerprints I'd already wiped off, why not leave a neat, if baffling, package for the police? Some amusing conversations would no doubt ensue when Davenport's finest tried to figure out how a guy with a .45 slug in his chest made it down all those floors and to the parking lot without being seen, and without dying first; ultimately, however, they would find the obvious explanation just too tidy to resist. Or, so I imagined. If they did tag me for it, they wouldn't get past the phony name I'd used at the desk, and I'd be long gone by then.

I picked her up at the front door, she got in, we drove away.

"Now," she said. "What is it makes you think somebody's out to kill me, anyway?"

"Oh," I said, looking at the Concort receding in the rear-view mirror, "I don't know."

19

"How much do you know about your husband's business dealings?" I asked her.

"He was an art dealer. He had money in an insurance agency. He was part owner of several mail-order businesses."

"That's not what I mean."

"You mean his illegal business dealings."

"That's right."

"Not much. Next to nothing."

We were past the city limits, on our way out of town, now. Traffic was light, but it was a foggy night, misting, and visibility was poor.

"Tell me as much as you do know, then," I said.

"While I was married to him, I thought he was a pillar of the community. Active in charity work. Chamber of Commerce, Lions Club, everything. He was conservative, politically. He wasn't active in local politics, not openly, anyway…he did have friends in political circles, and contributed heavily to various campaigns."

"You're talking about the public man, Carrie. What about the private man?"

"He was polite. Reserved. Kind. I know you're wondering about the age difference, and if you're thinking maybe he was more a father to me than a husband in some ways, yes, I suppose you're right. But he was a husband, too."

"Go on."

"When he was found murdered…shot to death, by the side of the road…" She stopped a moment, shivered. "…when that happened, I realized I'd been pretty naive. I realized there were things about him I hadn't known, that I'd been like a sheltered child where much of his life was concerned. Did you know that some narcotics were found in his possession? Or, rather in a locker at the airport that he had a key to. It was pretty obvious that he'd been involved in some kind of, what? Underworld activity. Sounds silly to say that, doesn't it?"

"No."

"Anyway, there were a lot of people with a lot of questions. Police, of course. Federal agents, because of the narcotics. More federal men, IRS, checking the books of my husband's various businesses. It only began cooling down this past month, and I don't anticipate it cooling down completely till who knows when."

"Are the federal men gone?"

"All but IRS. They haven't bothered me personally, much. The narcotics people and the police did, though. Unmercifully."

"Has anyone else come around to talk to you, Carrie? Someone who might claim to be an old business associate of your husband's."

"I haven't talked to anyone in the last three months

except members of my family and police and federal people. And you, Jack."

"And right now you're wondering how the hell to ask who the hell I am."

"Yes."

"Officially I was a salesman for one of those mail-order companies your husband was part owner of."

"Unofficially?"

"I guess you could say I delivered messages for him."

"You're being vague."

"I have to be."

"You're trying to say you were involved in the illegal side of what my husband did."

"Yes."

"I see. Then it wasn't accidental, our meeting each other?"

"I don't know."

"What do you mean?"

"I didn't arrange the meeting, Carrie. Did you?"

"No."

"Then we'll have to assume it was accidental."

"A coincidence, you mean."

"I used to stay at the Concort, whenever I came to the Cities on business, to confer with your husband. I like the Concort. I like to swim there. So when I came to the Cities this time, I stayed there again. And swam there again. You inherited an interest in the Concort when your husband was killed. You like to come around and swim there in the mornings. So we bumped into each other."

"That's still pretty coincidental."

"I know it is. It's the reason I didn't call you back today. I looked in your purse, last night, saw who you were. It bothered me. I wasn't going to contact you again till I was sure about you."

"Are you sure about me now?"

"I guess I have to be. Just like you have to be about me. Maybe we should just be tentatively sure about each other."

The fog and misting had us crawling along the highway. Few other cars were foolhardy enough to be out on a night like this, pushing through the thick, gray shifting unreality.

"You still haven't answered my question," she said.

"Which question?"

"Why do you think someone's trying to kill me?"

So I explained it to her, modifying certain parts and leaving others out, but giving her what was, essentially, the truth. I told her that an attempt had been made on my life, for reasons I had yet to ascertain, but that I had managed to trace the attempt to another former associate of her husband's (Ash) who I'd followed to the Quad Cities, where some sort of takeover of her husband's extralegal business activities seemed to be in progress, part of which involved Ash and another man staking out her home and recording her every move and, eventually, killing her.

I also told her that despite our poolside encounter, I hadn't known until a few hours ago that she was the potential victim in the brown brick house. And I told her that if she hadn't broken her usually rigid daily routine and driven to the Concort last night for an evening swim, she'd probably be dead now.

That chilled her a bit.

"I still don't understand why anyone would want to have me killed."

"Neither do I. I was hoping you could tell me."

"I can't. The part of my husband's life these people would be interested in, I'm totally ignorant of."

"Maybe they don't know that. Maybe you're in possession of information that could be dangerous to somebody, even if you aren't aware of it."

"I don't see how."

"Again, neither do I. But somebody does. Somebody considers you an obstacle. Somehow, you've got in the way of whoever it is who's trying to take over where your husband left off."

"And I don't even know what it is they're trying to take over. Narcotics smuggling? Crooked politics? What?"

"Do you really want to know?"

"No. No. No, I don't."

"Carrie, a while ago you said how those federal people and the police had bothered you…unmercifully, I think you said. Is that why you haven't asked me to take you to the police?"

"Oh, you're wondering if that's occurred to me. That I should be thinking, if my life's really in danger, shouldn't I run to the police? Why put myself in your hands instead, the hands of a stranger? Well, why not? Who else do

I have? I put myself in your hands last night, willingly enough. Why not again."

There was an uneasiness in her voice, despite her artificially flip attitude, that disturbed me. A resignation, that seemed to say, *If you're my lover, fine…but if you're my murderer, well that's fine, too…it just doesn't matter that much to me, one way or the other, anymore.*

"Carrie," I said. "If you think I've kidnapped you, you're wrong. If you want to go to the police, just say so. I'll turn this heap around and drop you off at the station in Davenport. Just say the word."

"No. No police. I told you about my husband's political ties. People in local government and beyond could be involved in the same illegal things he was involved in, and if there are people trying to kill me, it could very likely be them. So, no, I don't have the urge to call the police. But I would like to know what you hope to do for me. Besides hide me out for a while. How can you stop killers, anyway?"

"The same way they stop you."

"Oh. I think I see what you mean."

"Maybe you'll want to change your mind about the police, after all, Carrie. Knowing that."

"Knowing what? That some people are going to die? And that you're going to kill them? No. My husband was murdered. I'm apparently next on the list. People want to murder me. No, it doesn't bother me if people like that are killed. It doesn't even bother me if you're the one who does it. I just don't want to hear about it. Lie to me if you have to. But don't tell me."

We were coming into a small town, a cemetery on our left, a sign welcoming us to Blue Grass, population 1032, on the right.

"You might be holed up at that cottage several days," I said. "Got any food on hand there?"

"Not to speak of," she said.

"Well, if something's open here, we'll stop and pick some up."

A block later I pulled up along the curb in front of an old-fashioned clapboard grocery store and sent her in. Then I drove down another block and pulled in to get gas.

While the Buick was being filled, I went in and got change and used the pay phone.

I called the number Ash had given me earlier today.

The call went through immediately; one ring and a well-modulated baritone voice answered.

"Who's speaking?" I demanded.

"Curtis Brooks."

"Brooks, are you the man, or just a stooge? I don't want to talk to another go-between."

"You must be Mr. Quarry."

"Do you have ten thousand dollars handy?"

"Why?"

"Have it handy by tomorrow morning. Early. I've got the Broker's widow and that's what it'll cost you, if you want her."

I hung up, paid for the gas and drove over and picked her up at the grocery store, and we headed through the fog and mist toward her cottage.

20

I let her carry the groceries. There was only one bag and it didn't kill her. I carried the guns, the silenced Ruger I got off the dead backup man, and my .38, which I'd packed as a spare, the only thing I'd bothered to dig out of my suitcase for the stay at her cottage; the Ruger I kept in hand, the .38 I tucked in my waistband. And I did carry a six-pack of Coke, too, so don't get the idea chivalry's entirely dead.

Fifteen miles or so out of Blue Grass we had turned off the highway to cut over to the older highway that followed the river, and to do that we had to take side roads, gravel country roads that were winding and hilly and lined with trees, a journey that even under the best of conditions would have been a roller-coaster ride, let alone in this weather. So we didn't do much talking: I drove, and she helped navigate, and finally we came down a particularly steep hill and she pointed out the abandoned farmhouse she'd told me about, on the right-hand side of the road, near the bottom of the hill, just barely visible in the fog and looking like every kid's idea of a haunted house. She'd said this would make a good place to leave the car, and as I pulled in there I wondered for a second what she was leading me into, but she wasn't leading me into anything, as it turned out, except a good place to leave the car. With the Buick parked behind the sagging barn next to the deserted farmhouse, we set off through the fog on foot, her lugging the groceries, me the six-pack of Coke and guns.

We walked on the gravel road about a quarter-mile and then hit the highway, which immediately to our left was blocked, a sign on a fence-type barricade saying "Bridge Out—Detour," with an arrow pointing back the way we'd come, and flashing lights to make it all clearly visible even on a night like tonight. We skirted the barricade and followed the highway another quarter of a mile and then she led me off onto a graveled drive, which wound through a marshy area that was heavy on dead trees and strange shrubs and gnarled vines that stuck up out of and hovered over pools of water whose surfaces were as blotchy as a disease of the skin; it was a nice area, if you were looking for a preserve for water moccasins. Maybe that explained the privacy afforded a cottage that wasn't particularly fancy, just a little white house with a shingle roof, sitting way up on flood-precautionary stilts made of stacked cement blocks, above a snow-patched lawn that fell to the river and a modest dock; very ordinary looking, really, the sort of place you'd expect to see as one of a cluster of such cottages, not isolated, like this. Huddling around protectively were tall thick-trunked trees that didn't at all have the sinister appearance of the nearby swamplike area that gave this oasis its seclusion. There were wooden steps with rail along the side of the cottage, and she went up, and I followed, onto a sun deck. She put the grocery sack down to unlock the door and I asked her if this was the only entrance. She said it was. She asked if that was good or bad. I said probably good.

And it was. Unless somebody planned to set the place on fire or shoot tear gas in at us or something, having a single way in and out was a good thing. At this height, it would take mountain-climbing gear to come in a window anywhere but off that sun deck, where the front of the cottage made a sort of porch, with windows that were slatted, like oversize Venetian blinds made of glass, cranking shut from within and backed with screens and impossible to use for entry short of taking an ax to them. The only practical way into the place was through the front door, which, not surprisingly, is how we went in.

Stepping into the porch area, Carrie flicked on a standing lamp, explaining there was no overhead lighting at all inside, and I had a look around. The porch had a sofa and several soft-cushioned lawn chairs and a Formica-top table with chairs and a portable television on a stand and a braid rug on a tile floor. The walls were pine, though three sides of the room were dominated by those slatted windows; the back wall was decorated with framed prints of fishing and hunting scenes.

I asked Carrie if there'd been any trouble with vandalism, a lot of stuff in here to leave unattended, but she said before her husband died, he'd all but lived down here, keeping the place in use pretty much year round, and, too, the constable of a little town a few miles from

here kept an eye on the place, so seldom was it ever bothered. She doubted the constable would be around tonight,
though, what with the heavy fog and all, but if he was, she
could handle him.

If the porch area was the equivalent of a living room,
the larger, single room beyond was all the other rooms:
kitchen in the near right corner, off in a cubbyhole separate but unenclosed from the rest of the room, and off of
which was the john; a double bed in the far right corner,
next to a window; wood-burning stove (for heating purposes only) in the middle of the room, with stovepipe
rising through the low tiled ceiling; an informal office
area in the near left corner, just an old battered oak desk
with an equally battered wooden swivel chair; and a dark
pine trunk and several tall storage cabinets filling the rest
of the space along the walls, which were the same light
pine as the porch.

She put the groceries away while I built a fire. It was
cold in there, and we were both damp from our walk in
the mist, and I didn't figure a little chimney smoke was
going to attract any attention, in fog this dense.

So I sat feeding wood into the mouth of the stove, and
she came and sat on the floor next to me, getting close to
the warmth, watching the flames move. For a long time
her face was expressionless, blank, a mask the glow of the
fire began to play upon, making attitudes and emotions
and expressions seem to be there and then flicker away.

Maybe she was waiting to see if I'd brought her here
to kill her. Maybe I was thinking the same thing about

her. I did see her glance now and then at the guns, the Ruger on the floor between us, the .38 in my belt, but the meaning of her glance was elusive. She also looked at me, occasionally. Studied my face like she did the fire.

Then, suddenly, impulsively, she pulled her sweater over her head. She was wearing a skimpy, translucent bra, which she undid and let drop, and the shadows and colors of the fire reflecting off her flesh gave her an almost mystical look, like a textured photograph. She covered her breasts with her hands. She shook her head and the shoulder-length white-blond hair shimmered and caught glints of yellow and orange and copper, tossing them around like sparks. A grin glimmered across her no-longer mask of a face, and she opened her mouth and touched her tongue to her upper lip, then her lower, and then she grinned again, mouth still open, spreading her fingers over her breasts to let the nipples peek through. I reached out and touched her face, and her expression changed again, the smile disappearing, and something like pain crossed her features. She was cupping her breasts, now, offering them to me. I accepted.

We made love. We'd fucked in the pool, and screwed in bed, but this time we made love, on the cold tile floor, bathing in the heat and color of the fire, moving slowly together, slowly together, and after a long while warmth flooded into warmth, and then we were holding onto each other another long while afterward, the fire crackling and warning us it would die down completely if left unattended.

21

The Broker had his arm around her. She was wearing a bikini, the same white bikini she'd worn for me last night. Broker was in a blue sport shirt and tan pants and looked happier than I'd ever seen him, smiling so broadly the ends of his wispy mustache were sticking straight up. Carrie was smiling, too. They didn't look as wrong together as you might think. Broker never did look his age, despite his stark white hair and politician's bearing. And while Carrie was in her twenties, she could have been taken for older; it's difficult to pin down a woman's age, which is how they want it, I suppose.

Seeing them in the photograph together was a shock, somehow, and an involuntary twinge of resentment wormed its way through me, at the sight of this thick hand on her soft tanned shoulder. I'd accepted the fact that she'd been married to him, but an image of them together had never formed in my mind. And I'd instinctively chalked the marriage up as an arrangement, a marriage of convenience, and the obvious love between them shook me a little.

What got me wasn't Carrie, really. I already knew she was a sensitive type, able to feel loving toward just about anybody. But the Broker loving her, the Broker loving *anybody*, that was the surprise. I'd always assumed that behind his empty eloquence and stuffed-shirt demeanor there lurked something twisted and wrong. He was, after all, a man who fancied himself just another (very) successful businessman, and seemed bothered not a bit that his business was murder. Especially as long as people like me were around to carry it out for him.

No, it didn't seem right, the look of devotion, affection, and happiness on that self-important old bastard's face. Not right at all. I'd have been much less surprised to discover a photograph of him being whipped by some broad in black leather, or getting sucked off by one of the succession of young male bodyguards I saw him go through. I mean, surely the Broker was into something more kinky than just a younger woman. It was like finding the Boston Strangler shacked up with Miss America… the very wholesomeness of it was disgusting.

So was the idyllic atmosphere they were basking in. They were on a boat, a cabin cruiser apparently, fishing gear evident in the background of the color photograph, and lots of sun and blue sky.

"That was taken a year ago," she said. "In the Bahamas."

The picture was on the wall, with a number of other framed pictures of the Broker and Carrie, and of the Broker and various men and women I didn't recognize. I was sitting at the big scarred-top desk, flashing a high-intensity lamp on the wall of pictures, and had centered in on this one.

"You know," I said, "I saw you together once. I'd forgotten about it, just remembered. You were at a restaurant together, a fancy one, in the Quad Cities."

"When?"

"I don't remember exactly. Not too long ago." I *did* remember exactly, but didn't want to say; it was just days before the Broker died trying to have me killed.

"Did my husband introduce us?"

"No. I spoke to him, but not in front of you."

"How'd you manage that?"

"Wasn't hard. We met in the toilet. We talked in toilets a lot, your husband and me. It was that kind of relationship."

"Jack, I…I'd rather you didn't go into any of that. I…there are some things I'd really rather not know, Jack. I don't think I could handle knowing some things, you know?"

"Sure. Forget it. I didn't mean to bring any of that up, anyway."

"Listen, why…why don't I get us something to drink?" She was standing there in bra and panties with a plaid woolen blanket she'd got from somewhere shrugged around her shoulders.

Her eyes were big and clear and blue, and she looked like a kid. Funny, in that restaurant that time, I'd thought she was in her mid-thirties, thought she looked cold, the frigid bitch type, figured her for a wealthy, worldly, well-educated pain in the ass. Now, I knew she was in her late twenties and young for that, and anything but cold or a bitch, and no matter how many times she may have been to Europe or the Bahamas, worldly she wasn't, and no matter how many private schools for girls she'd suffered through, there was a lot this girl had yet to learn.

"I have bourbon in the cabinet," she said.

"Just put some Coke in a glass," I said. "Nothing hard for me."

She touched my leg and grinned in a way I hadn't seen since last night. "Maybe I'm in the mood for something hard."

"Maybe you better let me catch my breath," I grinned back. "For now, just some Coke and ice, okay?"

She went over to the kitchen area, dragging her blanket, and I flashed the little lamp across a few more pictures. Many of them were of the Broker and Carrie in shots similar to that one I'd lingered over, some of the photos taken here at the cottage and on the river, others sunny vacation pictures, the Bahamas, Florida, what-have-you. I skimmed right over one picture, thinking it was the Broker and Carrie with some unknown fellow vacationer, then something clicked in my head and I went back to it, lifted it in its frame off the wall, and gave it a close look.

The picture was of three people dressed in white tennis garb, rackets in hand, leaning against the wire-mesh fence of a court somewhere. One of them was the Broker, all right, but years ago. His face had never been lined, but it had gotten fleshy over the years, and in this picture his face was firm and lean, and his hair dark brown, with a few streaks of the premature white that would eventually take over. Next to him was a beautiful woman, who looked remarkably like Carrie, but was someone else, someone obviously related to her, an older sister perhaps. The woman was, in the picture, perhaps eighteen or twenty, and she had the same naturally white-blond hair as Carrie, only worn in the pageboy style of the times. It wasn't a color picture, but her eyes were light and clear and probably as blue as Carrie's, and only something slightly different around the nose and mouth made the woman less than a dead ringer for Carrie.

"My mother," she said, looking over my shoulder. She set the glass of Coke on the desk.

"Who's this next to her?" I asked, pointing at the guy on the woman's left. Broker was on her right.

"That's my father," she said.

"I see. Is there a story here?"

"I guess so. Sort of. Both of them loved her. They all three went to school together—college, I mean—back east someplace. My father ended up marrying her."

"And the other guy in the picture waited around a few years and then settled for you, is that it?"

"You make it sound sick or something…"

"Sorry."

"Maybe I can make you understand…"

"Please."

She didn't have the whole story, having just heard pieces of it, over the years. She gathered that her father and the Broker had been close friends before her mother came between them, and it wasn't until some few years later, with her mother's early death, that the two men resumed their friendship, perhaps out of a need to console each other. At any rate, she'd grown up having two fathers around, in a way, though the real one paid little attention to her ("He was busy, out of town on business a lot, still is…his firm handles cases all over the place"), though doting on her younger sister who didn't bear such a painfully close resemblance to their dead mother. Her surrogate father, however, the kindly old Broker, didn't shun Carrie for looking like her mother, rather his reaction was to worship the child for it. And she liked the attention of a doting father figure; she had settled for that, in lieu of the real thing. "I always told him I was going to marry him, when I grew up," she said, "and I did. And if you want to make something sick out of that, that's your problem."

She'd been frank with me, but there was one thing she'd sluffed over, and I had to go back to it, even at the risk of upsetting her further.

"Your mother," I said.

"What about my mother?"

"You said she died. You didn't say how."

"She was an alcoholic."

"That doesn't have to kill you."

"It did her. I was a little girl when it happened. She killed herself in a car."

"An accident."

"Or something. Look, I really don't want to talk about any of this anymore, if you don't mind. I mean, it's not really…relevant to anything, after all, is it? And, I…well, I have certain…wounds that never really healed over, in my life, you know? So don't ask me to go picking at them."

"Okay."

She dropped the blanket to the floor in a woolen puddle and sat on my lap and put her arms around my neck. "Why don't we go sit by the fire. It's going to die out if you don't tend to it."

"Let me ask you something first."

She sighed. Stiffened.

"I won't pick at any wounds," I said. "I promise."

"Go ahead and ask, then."

"Your husband…did he do much work down here, at the cottage? You said he was down here a lot."

"He was, and he did do some work down here, sometimes, but nothing important, I don't think. Just fiddled."

"What do you mean?"

"He just worked on minor stuff down here. Like his mail-order businesses. Checking the books and like that. He liked checking his own books. He had a streak of accountant in him. Now, are you going to keep that fire going or not?" She nuzzled my neck.

Earlier, after making love, she'd got me to take a shower with her, in this same coaxing way.

"You win," I said, and dumped her onto the blanket on the floor.

"Ouch! You're a bully."

I picked her up, blanket and all, and deposited her in

front of the dwindling fire. It didn't take long to get the fire going again, and she put her head on my lap, supposedly to go to sleep, but since my lap was her pillow she began smoothing it like one, and then pretty soon her head was in my lap, and then later, finally, she did fall asleep, curling into a fetal position, cuddling in against me, the blanket around her. I sat with her an hour watching the fire, not feeding it any more wood, letting it sputter and die, since the fog might lift and chimney smoke betray us.

She was sleeping soundly, now, and wouldn't be doing much complaining about me letting the fire go out, so I again lifted her in my arms, a heavy little bundle in her blanket, and took her over to the double bed and tucked her in.

Then I went back to the desk and started going through drawers.

22

A noise woke me, and for a moment I thought I was home, back in Wisconsin, and then I remembered where I was, in a cottage all right, but a different one, and on a river, not a lake. The circle had come around and this was ending as it began, with me waking up in the middle of the night, hearing somebody who was coming in to try and kill me.

Me and someone else, this time.

I was on the bed with Carrie, but not under the covers with her, just stretched out on my back, with all my clothes on, on top of the blankets, the silenced Ruger on my stomach, the .38 snug in my waistband. I hadn't really intended to fall asleep, but hadn't fought it either, despite the fact I was expecting a caller.

After all, I knew who my caller would be, and how he'd come in. Right now, for instance, he was working a key in the front door, just as I'd known he would. That wasn't the noise that woke me, though…it was the sound of him creeping up the outside steps; soundlessly, I suppose he thought. If so, he thought wrong. I'd heard him, and was awake, and by the time that key was slipping in the lock on the door, I was almost smiling.

I leaned over and put a hand across Carrie's mouth

and nudged her awake with my other hand, put my lips to her ear, and whispered, "We have company…be quiet, and don't panic."

The beam of a big heavy flashlight was probing the porch area, the door between the rooms having a window through which we could see our intruder and his light, though in the total darkness of the place he didn't see us yet. But he would soon.

Very soon, as now he was opening that door between rooms, that door with the window we'd been observing him through, and he stepped inside, into the room where we were on the bed in the far right corner, and I shoved Carrie off onto the floor, so she'd be between bed and wall and not in any line of fire, and took a couple of silenced shots with the Ruger at the source of the beam beginning to poke around the room.

By source I mean the flashlight itself, not the man carrying it, but I wasn't used to the Ruger and it was dark in there and I nicked his arm with one shot and I don't know where the other shot went, but the flashlight tumbled to the ground and some other metal thing did, too, as the guy slammed back against the door he'd just opened, then got the hell out and was clomping down those outside steps he'd come up so carefully minutes ago, before I was even off the bed.

Not that I was in a great hurry. I did get off the bed and turn to the window, which was right above where Carrie was on the floor, cowering, and I threw the lock and forced the window up and saw the guy running out there in the fog, which had thinned a bit, running off the gravel and splashing into the marshy area, an instinctive move I guess, an attempt to find a shortcut maybe, or lose himself as a target in the snarl of brush and branches and bog. All it served to do, of course, was slow him down, and he was hardly off the road, only a dozen feet from the house, when I yelled, "Ash!"

He froze a second, then trudged on a step.

He was well within range, and knew it, and I hardly had to yell at all when I leaned out the window and said, "Ash! You can stop, or I can stop you. Choose."

He chose to stop. He turned. Shrugged and grinned up at me, though as he shrugged the pain in his left arm where I'd nicked him made his grin turn into a wince. He walked back up onto the gravel of the drive and called up to me, "I'll wait here for you."

"You'll be covered from the window," I said, "so stay put while I come to you."

I tugged the .38 out of my belt and gave the gun to Carrie, who was still wide-eyed and quivering on the floor, back to the wall. She took it, but the gun lay in her palm like a stone, and she looked at it like she didn't know what the hell it was.

"Hey," I said. "Snap out of it."

She cupped the gun in both hands, pushed it toward me, her eyes pleading.

"You won't have to shoot at anybody," I said. "Just aim it at that guy out there till I can get to him. It'll take me a couple minutes to get there, because I don't know for sure he came alone, and I have to be careful and do it kind of slow. Okay? Now if he starts to run or anything, anything that seems wrong to you, fire the gun, but you don't have to aim it at him. The sound will stop him. I know him, and believe me, the sound will stop him just fine."

She sighed.

And I watched while she slowly, reluctantly, made her hand conform to the contours of the gun, and I lifted her off the floor by the waist, and she took the post at the window. Well, she was the prettiest backup man I'd ever had, anyway. Had to give her that much.

I went over and picked up the flashlight he'd dropped, and found that the other thing he'd dropped was a gun, the big .45 that went with the silencer I'd seen back at his motel room a couple days ago, and the silencer was on, and I wasn't surprised that this was the other thing he'd dropped. I put the flashlight on the desk and stuck the Ruger in my belt, in back, where it would be covered by the jacket I slipped on. I didn't want Ash to see the Ruger; he might recognize it. His .45 I kept in hand.

He had taken off the black thermal jacket he was wearing and was looking at where my slug caught him, as I approached.

"Bad?" I asked.

"No," he said. "Just a graze, but fuck, you could've killed me, Quarry, you know that?"

"Not could've. Should've."

"Aw, Christ, but you hold a grudge."

"Ash, I got no intention of standing out here in the cold listening to you explain how every time you try to kill me it's nothing personal."

"Well, it isn't, and I never tried to kill you in my life, Quarry, that's a fact."

"You sent people to do it last time, I know, so that one doesn't count. But what the hell do you call tonight?"

"Tonight?"

"You remember. A couple minutes ago. Think back."

"Yeah? Who shot at who? I didn't know you was in there. Shit. I thought it was crazy even to look down here, but I was told look, so I the fuck looked, is all. I didn't see a car, and there were no lights on, and I was…"

"Stupid?"

"That wasn't the word I was looking for but, yeah, I was stupid. And you're real smart. Now that that's settled, tell me…you got the broad in there, or not? She the one with the gun on me. Up in the window? Can she hear us talking?"

"Yes on all counts, except if you keep your voice down, she can't hear us."

"She wouldn't use that gun, would she?"

"Let me put it this way. She knows you were going to kill her last night, that you would have if you and your boy hadn't fucked up. And she knows you still want to kill her, if you can ever stop fucking up."

"I don't want to kill anybody, Quarry. I just got to make a living like everybody else."

"Fine. Sometime you really must tell me all about your

personal philosophy. But right now I got something else in mind for you. I want you to go wake up Brooks and tell him I have something he's looking for."

"The broad, you mean?"

"Not exactly. Oh, I have her, and she's still for sale, but she's part of a package deal. A twenty-thousand-dollar package."

"So what else is in the package?"

"A list."

"You know about that, huh? Well let me tell you something you don't know. My backup got himself killed tonight, and killed somebody himself while he was at it…some federal guy who was snooping in your hotel room, yes, your hotel room, some federal fucker who evidently was watching the broad, too, only we didn't know it before."

"Where do I send the sympathy card?"

"Chicago."

"Come again."

"That's who Brooks works for, in case you didn't know. The Family out of Chicago."

"You mean he represents them in court."

"I mean they own the son of a bitch."

"What's their interest in this? If Brooks is the new Broker, they wouldn't figure in. The Broker's operation isn't a Mafia thing."

"What you don't know, Quarry, would fill a book."

"Yeah, well so would what I know. Tell Brooks that. Tell him about the list, too. And the twenty thousand."

"Anything else, while I'm writing this down?"

"Tell him be in his office at six-thirty, with the twenty thousand. I'll let him know where he can take it and pay me and get his merchandise."

"Six-thirty. This afternoon."

"Six-thirty. This morning."

"That's a couple hours from now, Quarry! Where the fuck's he supposed to get twenty thousand by then?"

"Probably out of a wall safe."

Ash grinned. "Probably. I suppose you want me to go, now, right?"

"Right. Don't come back, or bother sending anybody back. We'll be gone. Anyway, before you make any move you're going to have to talk this over with Brooks, aren't you? And there isn't a public phone for miles, and besides, maybe he wouldn't want to hear about this on a phone, what with everything crawling with federal people, and..."

"All right, all right. You make your point. No funny stuff. Can I go?"

"Go."

He went.

And I went back and told Carrie to get her clothes on.

"First take this," she insisted, handing me back the .38, shuddering, like somebody squeamish who'd been made to handle a snake.

I took the gun, put it back in my belt, and said, "I got to get you to a motel, somewhere out of the way, till this is over."

"When?"

"When what?"

"Will this be over?"

"Oh. Soon. It'll be over soon."

That seemed to ease her mind, and she got herself moving again. Which was the desired effect, of course.

Not that I'd been lying, when I said it would be over soon. It would be.

I just hoped she wasn't expecting a happy ending.

23

The fog had lifted. Dawn was maybe an hour away, so the streetlights were still on, reflecting off pavement made slick by eight or nine hours of misting. I left the Buick in the parking ramp, which at this hour was all but empty, across from the Conklin Building in downtown Davenport. I was alone. Under my arm was a large manila envelope, which I'd found in the scarred-topped desk at the cottage. My corduroy jacket was slung over my right forearm, covering the hand with Ash's silenced .45 in it. I crossed the street.

The bottom floor of the Conklin Building was taken up, primarily, by a motion picture theater, the last surviving such theater in the business district, not counting various porno houses on the fringes. The theater was not at all rundown, in fact had obviously had its face lifted not long ago; but the rest of the Conklin Building was no great shakes. It was a white stone building that had long since turned dingy gray, whose only distinction was twelve stories, ranking it among the tallest of buildings in this modest Midwestern downtown.

Not that it was shabby, but neither was it what I expected of a building where Curtis Brooks, nationally prominent attorney, would keep his office. Surprising, too, was the absence of any junior or other partners; Brooks, despite his fame (or infamy) in his profession, was alone in his practice. This I discovered as I studied the registry in the cubbyhole that served as a lobby for the Conklin Building, just an entryway leading to an elevator, which I stepped into, punching the button marked 12, Brooks's floor.

When the elevator door opened, Ash was waiting for me.

We didn't say anything to each other, even though I had said (or implied) I'd contact Brooks by phone rather than come in person. Ash wasn't surprised to see me, and I wasn't surprised by his lack of surprise. He walked me down an echoing corridor, lined with flat colorless, plaster walls, wood doors with steamy pebbled glass panes with black lettering, doctors, insurance agents, lawyers. I wondered how many teenage girls had walked the corridors of this building, on their way to have a quiet little illicit abortion.

At the dead-end of the corridor the pebbled translucent glass read: "Curtis Brooks, Attorney at Law."

Ash opened the door, but I waited for him to go in first. The reception room was dark, small, unpopulated, reasonably well-appointed but nothing fancy. To the rear of the room, behind the receptionist's desk, were two doors, one of them standing open to reveal a small law library, four walls of books, room enough to walk around but that's all. The other door was closed, and I waited for Ash to open it and go in, and then followed.

This room was barely larger than the outer office. It too was well-appointed: dark paneling, green shag carpet, leather couch against one wall, several chairs, big, imposing mahogany desk. The most interesting thing in the room was the oil painting on the wall over the couch. It was a painting of a beautiful middle-aged woman.

The second most interesting thing was Brooks himself, sitting in the high-backed swivel chair, half-turned and looking out the sheer-curtained window behind his desk, not blinking, let alone speaking at our entrance. He still seemed smaller than he should, but I had to admit he had a certain presence, like a movie star who can't act but somehow commands your attention, anyway. The deep tan, the character lines in all the right places, the wavy brown hair with white around the ears, the intense brown eyes, the expensive suit he wore even for a six-thirty-in-the-morning appointment with the likes of me, all conspired to make him as imposing a figure as the desk he loomed behind.

On that desk, which was otherwise empty but for a phone, was a briefcase. Not turning toward us, Brooks reached a hand over and flicked the latches on the briefcase and it yawned open, revealing neatly stacked and tightly packed rows of green, banded packets of cash.

"There," Brooks said, "is your money." His baritone was almost bored; no courtroom flair at all.

I reached in my pocket and took out a key. Brooks turned, finally, his chair turning with him; he wanted to see what I was doing.

I was handing the key to Ash.

"Cozy Rest Motel," I said. "Highway 6, past the city limits a few miles."

Brooks waved a finger at Ash. "Go," he said. Ash hesitated.

"Well?" Brooks said.

Ash said, "You…want me to leave you here?"

"We aren't going with you," Brooks said. Sarcastic. Impatient.

"Well…okay. But what do I do with…?"

"Do what you should have done two nights ago."

Ash made a whatever-you-say face and left. I pulled a chair around in front of the desk, closed the lid on the briefcase.

"Is there twenty thousand here?" I asked.

"Frankly," Brooks said, "no. There isn't. More like ten."

"Well. I only gave you half of your package, anyway."

"When I see your…list," he said, "you can have the rest."

"You don't believe I have it."

"No."

"Then why are you sitting here with me in your office, at six-thirty Saturday morning, your day off…pushing a briefcase of money at me."

"For that motel-room key you gave Ash. Nothing more."

"You're not pretending there's no list, are you?"

Polite laugh. "I'm not even sure I know just what sort of a list you're talking about, Mr. Quarry."

"Oh. You want to know how much I know, before committing yourself further. You want to know how much I've figured out."

He shrugged with his eyebrows, and as I looked at his eyes I saw that this casual manner was a pose. The eyes looking out of the shell that pretended to be relaxed and even disinterested spoke instead of urgency and even desperation. And something else. A flicker of something else. Fear?

"You were the Broker's business partner," I said. "A silent partner. You provided financial backing for him and shared in the revenue of his business. Oh, you weren't actively involved in that business…but you knew what it was about…you knew murder was the commodity Broker dealt in."

He was beginning to smile, now, just a little.

"For some reason, though, Broker kept you in the dark about some parts of the business. Maybe he anticipated you might try and take over the operation, if you had half a chance…half a chance, and his list."

"This list again. And again I must ask: What sort of a list is it, exactly?"

"A master list, you might say."

"And just what is on this 'master list'?"

"Not what. Who."

"All right, Mr. Quarry. We've come this far. I'll ask… *who* is on the list?"

"Me. And around fifty other people like me. Many here in the Midwest, but others all around the country, too. Names. More than names…dossiers, really. The people who pulled triggers for Broker. People willing to kill, for a price."

A small pearl of sweat was moving down his forehead.

He touched a finger to it and said, "Of what value would such a list be to me?"

"You're the new Broker. Or, you want to be. You need the list, to be in business."

"I see. And you have it. The list."

I let him see the manila envelope. The outside of it, that is. Didn't hand it to him. Just let him see.

And I also dropped the corduroy jacket down into my lap, to let him see Ash's gun in my hand, in case he'd had any doubt it was there.

"Your price," Brooks said, the faintest tremor in his voice, "is fair. In fact, asking only ten thousand more is more than fair, considering the value to me that list holds. This I freely admit to you. I also freely admit I do not have the money."

"What?"

"It's the truth. I simply don't have it. The time element isn't the problem, either. The money's just not there."

"Brooks, ten thousand, twenty thousand, *fifty* thousand, ought to be nothing to you."

"It ought to be. It isn't. I can offer you something else, something potentially far more profitable…"

"Ash's chair, you mean? No thanks."

"What *do* you want, then?"

"Suppose all I wanted was the answers to a couple questions. Suppose I'd settle for that, and the money in the briefcase."

"I wouldn't believe you."

"You're not in a position not to believe me."

"True. In that case, I'd accept your terms."

"Those are my terms."

"Then ask your questions."

"You can start by explaining why you tried to have me killed."

"Complexity of reasons. As a precautionary measure, if nothing else. Did you know we had your lake home in Wisconsin watched, for several months? And it was searched, thoroughly, more than once. We needed to know if you had the list. We knew 'the Broker,' as you call him, had gone to meet you on the night of his death, for which we assumed you were responsible, and…"

"You keep saying we…"

"Oh. You're wondering if I mean the editorial 'we'? I mean Ash and myself. I had been using Ash as a personal bodyguard, off and on, for about a year…I have periodic threats on my life, thanks to the nature of my courtroom activities…he was, you might say, and as you may have guessed, on loan to me by your Broker, after whose death I would never have been able to even attempt picking up the pieces without Ash. Without Ash, I would have had no direct connection to your end of this business, Mr. Quarry."

"Ash knew Broker had gone to see me the night he died, is that it?"

"Precisely."

"Has Ash told you, since talking to me, that I didn't kill the Broker? That Broker tried to have *me* killed, and got it from his own man in the process? That your precious fucking list had nothing to do with it?"

"Yes, but at the time we assumed differently. We assumed the list had everything to do with it, and took the steps I've already mentioned…watching your home, searching it…"

"If I'd had the list, what good would killing me have done?"

"First of all, Ash advised not having you tortured, to find out what you knew. He said, in effect, you were just perverse enough to lie in the face of death, especially an inevitable one. He also said killing you point-blank was a better idea than forcing a confrontation, which you might be able to squirm out of."

Ash knew me pretty well.

"After your death," Brooks continued, "all of your property would have gone to your family, who would have no knowledge of the nature of your line of work, and from whom the list could easily be bought, stolen, or coerced. If you think that is far-fetched, I can tell you the city and street address of your parents in Ohio, Mr. Quarry. Our research has been most thorough, I assure you."

"I'm impressed," I said, honestly. "Suppose I'd been hired to kill the Broker, by somebody else after the list, somebody who wanted to take over Broker's operation just like you do."

He was beginning to enjoy himself. Smiling. "Killing you might flush out whoever that somebody else might be, in that event. If we had competition, we wanted to know who it was. And if you had killed him for some other reason, some personal reason, you were still a dangerous loose end that needed tying off…as you have so ably proven, with your presence here these past few days."

He reminded me then of the Broker, sitting there with his hands calmly folded across his chest, slight smirky smile on his face, the picture of respectability, having a fine time telling of the intricate and self-centered schemes he'd cooked up, schemes that included murder and anything else it took to get ahead, to be successful.

It was no wonder they were friends and business associates. It was no wonder they'd been friends at that college back east, even sharing the same lover, the beautiful woman who even now was looking down from the oil painting across the room, that portrait of a woman whose hair was blond and pulled back away from a face that in life probably had not grown older as gracefully as the artist indicated, though he'd captured a great sadness in the familiar blue eyes.

"Okay," I said. "That explains why you tried to have *me* killed. But what about Carrie. Explain that to me, Brooks. Why are you trying so hard to kill your daughter?"

24

He clapped his hands together once, not loud, just a "well!" gesture, and said, "I suppose you sent Ash to an empty motel room."

"That's right."

"Surely you don't expect me to be surprised to find you know I'm the girl's father. You had plenty of time with her to learn that, what with all the questions you must have asked her...though I admit your failure to mention it till now had me assuming perhaps you *didn't* know, which seemed possible, since my daughter and I share a singularly empty relationship, making it somewhat unlikely she'd mention me, without some prodding from an outside source like yourself, that is. No matter. Why don't we go on to more important things."

"Than killing your kid, you mean."

"Ash *did* tell you about the federal agent who was killed last night? In your room at the Concort? You *do* understand the implications of that?"

"Sure. It's going to get hot around here."

"*Understatement as a Way of Life*...if you ever write a book, Mr. Quarry, that should be the title...*Understatement as a Way of Life.* It is, indeed, going to get hot around here. Soon. Today."

"Something you can't handle, is it?"

"The police I can handle. The federal investigators, hopefully, will not be a major problem, since their man died in an exchange of fire with another man, who died himself in that same exchange. Still, an investigation of the magnitude federal people could conceivably exert will make some...friends of mine in Chicago somewhat...nervous. Yes. Chicago is another question entirely."

"What's Chicago got to do with anything? Broker's operation was never a syndicate thing. You represent them in court, I know, but so what?"

"I wish my involvement with my friends in Chicago was as casual...as voluntary...as you suggest."

"But it isn't?"

"No, Mr. Quarry. You see...what's the best way to put it? They own me. The handsome fees you must think I receive are a figment of the public's imagination. I am given an allowance, like a child. Occasionally I'm given permission to handle an outside case, for appearance sake. The money I do receive is just enough to maintain a certain level, a front, a facade. But nothing lavish. Surely you wondered about this office, and my lack of associates, distinguished or otherwise? I don't even own my home, Mr. Quarry; a corporation does. And you can guess who owns the corporation."

"How did it happen?"

"I owed them a lot of money. I was a young man, recently married, with a child, a promising career, and... gambling debts. Yes, I owed them a lot of money. I traded them my life for it. Those, literally, were the terms."

"Then I was wrong…?"

"Wrong in guessing I was your Broker's silent partner? Only in that you assumed I backed him financially. Hardly. What I did for him was help him build his own facade, here in the Quad Cities, where I enjoy a certain amount of respect and social standing. I let him bask in that, share it. And one other thing. I was his link. To the people in Chicago. His 'clients'…came from me."

"You."

"Me. Where did you suppose your Broker found his clients? On the street? By advertising? How do you suppose people knew to turn to him with their…problems? Think about it. Take your average semi-respectable businessman, who wants someone out of the way…his wife, his mistress, a business rival, a business partner, a troublesome politician, anyone. To whom does a man with such a need, such a problem, turn? Well, being a businessman, he has, in the course of business, most likely come in contact with an occasional acquaintance who just might happen to have a link or two to so-called organized crime. He goes to this acquaintance, in confidence, discusses his problem, hypothetically, of course…and he asks his acquaintance, with the sinister connections, 'Whom might one turn to if one wanted someone killed?'"

"And the guy with the problem eventually gets referred to a Broker, is that it?"

"That's it exactly," Brooks said, nodding smugly. "You see, Mr. Quarry, it's convenient for my friends in Chicago to have people like yourself on tap, so to speak…it's occasionally necessary for them to make use of outside people, for housecleaning, among other things, and they keep such people prosperous and thereby available by maintaining them, through a sort of referral service. Can you claim you've never been involved in a syndicate-related job? Of course, you can't. Now, I've been generalizing here, naturally, and have been necessarily vague about the finer points, but you now have an idea, at least, of how the business you've been involved in for some years actually works. The cog finally begins to understand the wheel."

"Didn't you make any money feeding Broker clients?"

"Yes. My involvement in this particular, somewhat distasteful business arrangement was the sole crumb thrown me by my Chicago friends. Here, at last, I was allowed to pursue a dishonest dollar like any good American."

"Then why are you still hurting for cash?"

"Because I made some decisions, relating to the stock market, which were no wiser than decisions I made years ago, when I gambled in less socially acceptable ways."

"You're still losing, you mean."

"I wasn't losing, Mr. Quarry, not in this situation, anyway, until you turned up on the scene."

"You seem to think you're going to lose where Chicago's concerned."

"Possibly. But I really think I can handle that. They won't be happy about the death of that federal man, true, but as I explained to you, and will explain to them, that's a storm we all should be able to weather. Still, it will be an effort to convince them I haven't hopelessly botched my attempt to reopen your Broker's referral service. Knowing I had the list would soothe them, a bit, however."

"It means that much to you."

"Enough to kill my own child, you mean?" He sighed, heavily, and the well-etched character lines in his browned face seemed to sag a little, for the first time. "Pay attention, Mr. Quarry, and I will do my best to once and for all satiate your seemingly unquenchable need to know. You may not be aware that my late wife was the only child of a rather wealthy industrialist, here in the area. That brown brick home you've been spending so much time watching of late is only one of several my wife's parents maintained. You may be wondering why my wife's parents didn't, uh, bail me out, when I had my gambling debts to settle. They could have, but refused. My wife felt similarly. She was obsessed with the idea I married her for her money, when actually, that was only part of it. Nevertheless, there is a great deal of money there, that for many years has been just beyond my reach. Now. Do you understand, finally? I know that *I* will *never* understand your need to know these things, seeing as God alone knows how many men died at your hands while you had no notion at all of why they were dying. No, I will never understand what has suddenly turned you into someone so curious no stone must be left unturned, for fear some bug or snake or other crawling thing might escape your sight."

He must have been something in front of a jury, pleading the life of some syndicate asshole. He could do things with words, pull them right out of his head and stick them in the goddamnedest sentences, without any apparent effort. I could see why the syndicate people had wanted him. He used logic and words as mindlessly, and effectively, as any gunman pulling a trigger.

Just the same, I felt he'd told me the truth, just now. It made too much sense, felt too much like something somebody like him or the Broker would do, for it to be anything else but the truth. If his daughter died, everything would go to him: not only the list, if she'd had it—as, unwittingly, she had—but all of the Broker's business interests, the legal and extralegal alike, and all of his dead wife's family's wealth, and for the first time he'd have a financial life of his own; he could continue to repay his endless debt to the Family in Chicago, in court, but he'd no longer be a monetary prisoner; he could pursue the good life, whatever the hell his notion of a good life might be. Whatever it was, it sure didn't include his daughter.

"You want the list," I said.

"You know I do."

"Then I want you to do one thing more for me, and it's yours."

"Name it."

"I have a phone number I want you to dial. You'll be calling Carrie. It's the phone in a motel room where she really is waiting. I want you to call her and say, 'I'm sorry, for everything,' and hang up. Make sure she knows it's you."

"This won't change anything about what I feel has to be done about her…there's no way around that…"

"That's okay. Let's just ease her mind."

"You amaze me. Sentiment?"

"Just do it, if you want your fucking list."

He stared at me, but all he saw was a poker face, and he couldn't read it; he just wasn't a very good gambler and that's all there was to it.

I watched him dial. I had him hold the phone away from his ear a little so I could hear her.

"Yes?" she said, answering.

"Carrie, this is your father. I want you to know I'm sorry, for everything."

And he hung up.

"Good," I said. "Now, here's your list."

I opened the manila envelope and dumped its contents on the desk.

His eyes were very wide as he looked at the ashes heaped before him. You'd think somebody had tipped over an urn full of a favorite relative's cremated remains, though in Brooks's case, I doubted he had any favorite relatives, not unless you counted those he wanted to inherit money from. He touched the ashes with the fingers of one hand, sifting, searching, then slapped his hand against them, hard, and dark flakes floated in the path of the rays of dawn just peeking in the window behind him.

"The list," he said.

I nodded.

"All yours," I said.

He surprised me. I didn't think he had it in him, but he lunged forward, sliding across the top of the desk, knocking the phone jangling to the floor, knocked me and the chair I was sitting in back and onto the floor, and he was on me, his hands on my throat, and I cuffed him on the ear with the .45 and pushed him off.

"That…that call I made," he said. "It was…a suicide note, wasn't it?"

"Don't cause me any more trouble, and it'll go easier for you."

"You want to know the funniest part? She wasn't even my daughter, Quarry. She wasn't even mine."

I didn't know what he was talking about, and I didn't want to know. He was defeated now, just a slack sack of humanity, of a sort, anyway. He didn't cause any more trouble. I kept my word. I kicked him in the head, and he was unconscious when I took him over to the window, opened it, and threw him out.

25

The Cozy Rest Motel was everything its name promised, and less. The office was just one of a dozen and a half individual huts covered with sheets of pink pseudo-brick. In the office window was a Christmas tree, a little plastic one on a table, and a frowzy fat woman was decorating it with tinsel. A tinny speaker hanging from a nail over the door was spitting Christmas music, and it was still November, for Christsake. The rest of the cabins were in the wooded area behind, united by a gravel road that curved around like a drunken snake, through trees that had to look better than this during some season. It was cold again this morning, and the snow that hadn't melted yesterday was clumped and misshapen and hard-crusted, looking like chunks of Styrofoam randomly scattered around the gray ground the cabins overlooked.

Ash was in number two.

I'd left him a note on the dresser saying, "I lied. Wait for me and I'll tell you all about it. It's too late for you to do anything else, anyway."

He was waiting. Sitting on the lumpy bed in the dreary little cabin, whose wallpaper walls were peeling to reveal other, even uglier wallpaper.

"Oh, it's you, Quarry," he said. He gestured to the four

tight walls around him. "I was expecting Bonnie and Clyde."

"Brooks is dead."

"Yeah, well, I figured. Where you got the broad hid?"

"Doesn't matter. It's all over."

"Not if you really got the list, it isn't. We can go in together. I didn't trust Brooks that much, anyway."

"That was smart. He tried to get me to kill you and take your place."

"That fuckin' little pimp shyster. What'd you do to him?"

"Tossed him out the window."

"Good for you. He wanted a fall guy, well, he got one. Hey, not a bad sensa humor on the kid, huh? So what about the list?"

"I had it. I burned it."

"Burned it! Je-sus Christ! You got any idea what that mother was worth?"

"I don't care. I got no desire to play Broker."

"Well, fuck, *I* do!"

"Anyway, I didn't like all the stuff about me that was down in black and white. And about you, and a lot of guys like us."

"Quarry! That was like burning money."

"Well, it's gone now."

"Jesus, Quarry."

"You should thank me. That list fell into the wrong hands, your ass and mine and a lot of people would've been in one fine sling."

"I suppose. But shit."

"You want your gun back?"

"My .45, you mean? Please."

I gave it to him.

"Bulky son of a bitch, ain't it?" he said. "That federal fucker had one, you know, with a silencer too, even. Silencers are illegal as shit, what's a federal fucker doing with one, I mean, what's the goddamn country coming to. You know…you could've killed Brooks with this, and set me up for it."

"I know. I didn't."

"Well, while I'm not exactly thrilled you burned my future up for me, you bastard, I got to thank you for giving me an out."

"What are friends for."

"Right. Looks like I owe you another one."

"Let's just say this one's on me and leave it go at that."

"Anything you say. I suppose you made it look like suicide?"

"Yeah."

"I'll let on like I figure that's what it was, if the mob guys ask me, and they will. Well. Nothing to hang around this dump for. Shit. First thing, I'm going to have to unload that fuckin' LTD on somebody and get something cheaper to drive."

"Got any other plans?"

"No. I don't know. What the hell. There's other Brokers around, you know. I suppose I'll find one and stay in the business. What about you?"

"I don't know."

"Maybe I'll see you sometime."

"Maybe."

I watched him walk out to his car. He waved before he got in. I waved as he left. Maybe I would see him again. I hadn't burned the list, of course. Those ashes I dumped on Brooks's desk were just some papers I burned in the wood-burning stove down at the cottage. But I wanted it to filter back to Chicago, through Ash, that the list was gone. I didn't want anyone thinking I had it, because I had plans for it.

And I knew why Ash and Curtis Brooks hadn't been able to find the list. It wasn't a list at all, really. Certain people on the payrolls of Broker's businesses (the mail-order ones, like the lingerie company I "worked" for) were coded in a way that matched up with certain slides in little yellow boxes that otherwise contained memories of various vacations Broker had been on. There was a whole pine chest packed with these boxes of slides, and only by going through every one of thousands of slides would you be able to find the less than fifty that counted, which were not really slides at all, though mounted like the rest; they were a type of microfilm, a single panel of microfilm with photographs and documentary material on forty-eight individuals, of which I was one, and Ash another. On the cardboard-mounting material were the number/letter combinations that coincided with names on master payroll lists from the mail-order businesses. I'd been up almost all night, piecing this together. I wasn't about to burn any of it, except for my own card.

But I really didn't want to be the Broker, and I wasn't going to blackmail anybody, either...professional killers aren't the best people to try to blackmail. What I had in mind was something different. A one-man operation.

Life is a precious commodity. People will pay a lot to have one taken. But they will pay even more to hang onto one...if it's their own. This was the profit angle Ash hadn't been able to see. All he could see (and Brooks, too) was the killers. I could see the victims. People like Carrie, who without help were going to die.

As Ash pointed out, there were other Brokers. Most of the hitmen (and women) named here would be working again, soon, if not already, for new Brokers. If I picked a name from the list, followed whoever it was to a job, found out who the potential victim was, I could go to that potential victim and offer my services. If my offer was rejected, no skin off my ass; let the asshole die, it's up to him. Some might prefer to go to the cops, though in most cases people lined up to be hit can't go to the cops, because the hit usually has something to do with some less than legal activities the victim's been mixed up in.

But some *would* take me up on my offer, and be willing to pay my fee, in which case I'd prevent the hit, killing those sent to do it and doing my best in the process to find out who hired them, and possibly take care of who ever that was, too.

At least it was something to think about. An idea, anyway, something to consider while I sat staring at the

frozen lake in Wisconsin this winter, waiting to see if the
federal snoopers would trace those Concort killings to
me, which would cause me to have to start from scratch:
new name, new residence, new face maybe, the works.
That was a bridge I'd cross if I came to it.

In the meantime, I'd consider this new idea, an idea I
liked a lot better than that of working for somebody else.
I'd had it with that scene. I didn't want to work for anybody, and I didn't want anybody working for me. Of course,
I'd still be killing people, but for the most part it would
just be other hitmen, like myself, and that seemed a step
up, somehow.

26

Carrie was in number 9.

"Jack," she said. "The strangest thing…my father called me…here!"

"I know," I said.

I had her sit on the bed.

"I went to see him," I said, hands on her shoulders. "We had a long talk. Before I left, he asked me if I knew how he could get in touch with you. I gave him the number. What did he say to you?"

She told me.

"I kind of thought it would be something like that," I said. "Carrie, your father killed himself."

"Wh…what?"

"I was barely out of the building. A small crowd was gathering on the sidewalk…it was just after dawn…he'd thrown himself out of his office window. I'm sorry."

"Why…why on earth would…?"

"He had connections to organized crime. You probably know that. So did your late husband. You know that, too. Your father found out that some syndicate people from Chicago were trying to have you killed."

"Me? Why?"

"You inherited some business interests from your husband that the Chicago people wanted to see in your father's hands. Killing you would have made that possible. Your father knew that, and must have figured the only way to stop it was to kill himself, and in so doing end the need for anyone wanting to kill you."

She was crying by now, of course.

"This is going to be difficult for you, I know. There'll be a lot of questions, from a lot of quarters. Just tell the truth, tell them what your father called and said, tell them about me, that we spent some time together, at the Concort, at the cottage. Don't mention that I worked for your husband, though. Better say I was, you know, just a casual pickup. Better not show any knowledge of any of this mob stuff, either, that killers were after you, none of that. Otherwise you could cause problems for yourself and maybe me."

"Will you…stay with me…help me through this?"

"I can't. I think you can understand why."

She threw her arms around my waist and sobbed into my chest. This went on for some time.

Finally, I got her out into the Buick and went over all of it again for her, several times, as I drove into town. She was still crying, but now and then she would ask a question about the story I'd told her and I'd give her as good an answer as I could. She seemed to buy it all.

Then, as I glanced at her, turning down Brady toward downtown, I noticed something about her I'd never noticed before. She had just the slightest resemblance to somebody, somebody I used to know. And some things suddenly made a crazy kind of sense to me, or maybe I *was* crazy, but I thought about the two college guys who, back east some years ago, had loved the same woman; and then one of them evidently faded away for a time, for some reason or other, while the other married the girl, partially for money, partially perhaps because she was pregnant with Carrie, which according to Carrie's age would have been about right; and then the mother had developed a drinking problem and sad, sad eyes and died; after which the father, Curtis Brooks, couldn't stand the sight of his daughter, because she reminded him of his wife, the resemblance was that striking, and yet Brooks had kept the wife's portrait hanging in his office...

He'd said something strange to me, before I killed him.

"I wasn't even her father..."

Then who was?

I never did see the inside of that brown brick castle. Just as I never would understand what had gone on in there. I didn't know what the furniture was like, whether the colors were lively or somber; I didn't know what the relationship was like, whose personality dominated, or did they share and share alike. I didn't want to know, either.

Maybe it was just my imagination that made me suddenly see a resemblance between the Broker and Carrie; anyway I kind of hope it was.

But before I dropped her off at the Concort, where her car was still in the lot, she said, "Maybe…maybe in his own way, my father did love me."

Maybe she didn't know how right she was.

Afterword

Quarry was an accidental series character. He has been called the first hitman to helm a crime-fiction series, and I think he probably is, and of course I'm glad to be heralded as an innovator. But as with Quarry, my distinction is somewhat accidental.

The first novel, *Quarry,* begun at the University of Iowa Writers Workshop around 1971, was designed to be a one-shot. A standalone. My protagonist was left at the conclusion in a fairly untenable position—it seemed clear that, sometime after the final page turned, he would be killed by people like himself.

Earlier I had written a novel called *Bait Money* about a thief who died on the last page. I had also written a novel called *No Cure for Death* about a mystery writer who got himself entangled in a real murder case. Obviously *Bait Money* wasn't conceived as a series, or I wouldn't have killed Nolan; and had I wanted to do more novels about Mallory, I would have given him a better job description than, well, mystery writer.

But I was lucky enough to have an editor request more books about both characters. Nolan had remained killed when the sixth or seventh editor to look at (and reject) *Bait Money* had spilled coffee on the manuscript. My then-agent Knox Burger, who had never liked the ending, said that since I had to retype "the goddamn thing" anyway, I might as well put a better ending on. So Nolan's sidekick Jon swooped in to save him, in a Batman and Robin tradition that suited the book. Should I have typed "spoiler alert" before revealing that? Since seven more Nolan novels have appeared since, I think it's safe to reveal he no longer dies at the end of *Bait Money*.

The Mallory character solved a few more murder mysteries before the weight of his improbability crushed us both. But there was kind of a half-assed logic to a mystery writer getting involved in mysteries. Worked for Jessica Fletcher (and still does for her ghost writer, Donald Bain), and I even later wrote a series of novels about real-life famous mystery writers who got involved in murder investigations.

Quarry, however, I had left in a real jam. So when I was asked to do more novels about him (notice I never have any artistic misgivings about writing sequels to novels that were conceived as one-shots), I realized the next book would essentially have to be devoted to getting him out of that jam.

Also, since Quarry's agent in the murder business, the Broker, was deceased, I needed a new conduit for Quarry to have further jobs. I came up with the notion of the Broker's list, which fueled a number of the later novels, and added the interesting resonance of Quarry tracking other killers like himself. Sort of surrogate suicide.

My original title for this novel was *Hit List*, which in

1975 was a fresh idea. Once again, the publisher changed my title without consulting me (they had published *Quarry* as *The Broker*), and the novel appeared in 1976 as *The Broker's Wife*. I despised that title (still do) because it gives away a major plot point. "Spoiler Alert" should have appeared on the cover. Anyway, when Foul Play Press, in the mid-'80s, republished the first four Quarry novels, I changed the title to *Quarry's List*. And so it remains.

The pattern of using Quarry's name in the titles seems to have stuck, and the new entries in the series published by Hard Case Crime in recent years have followed it. The new books have generated interest in the old ones, and I am grateful to Hard Case Crime for making all of the Quarry novels available under one imprint.

MAX ALLAN COLLINS

WANT MORE QUARRY?

Try These Other Quarry Novels From
MAX ALLAN COLLINS and
HARD CASE CRIME

Quarry

When a job goes horribly wrong, Quarry sets out to find out who hired him—and take revenge.

Quarry's Deal

Quarry's plan to target other hitmen for elimination hits a snag when he comes up against a deadly female assassin.

Quarry's Cut

It's not unusual to see bodies on the set of an adult film, but when they're *dead* bodies, Quarry has his work cut out for him.

Quarry's Vote

Happily retired, Quarry turns down a million dollars to assassinate a presidential candidate. But it's not the sort of job you can just walk away from…

Read On for the
Opening Chapters of
QUARRY'S DEAL!

1

I waited for her to come, and when she did, so did I. I asked her to lift and she lifted and let me get my hands out from under her. Here I'd been cupping that ass of hers, enjoying that fine ass of hers, and then we both came and suddenly her ass weighs a ton and all I can think about is getting my hands out from under before they get the fuck crushed.

I rolled off her.

"Was it good for you?" she asked.

"It was fine."

There was a moment of strained silence. She wanted me to ask, so I did: "How was it for you?"

"Fine," she said.

That taken care of, I got off the bed, slipped into my swim trunks, trudged into her kitchen, and got myself a bottle of Coke.

"Get some Kleenex for me," she called from the bedroom.

I was still in the kitchen. I said, "You want something to drink?"

"Please! Fix me a Seven and Seven, will you?"

Jesus, I thought. I put some Seagram's and Seven-Up and ice in a glass, got her some Kleenex from the bathroom,

...d went into the bedroom, where she took both from me, ...etting the glass on the nightstand, stuffing the Kleenex ...between her legs.

There was a balcony off the bedroom, through French doors, and I went out and looked down on the swimming pool below. It was mid-evening, and cool. Florida days are warm year round, they say, but the nights are on the chilly side, particularly a March one like this.

Not that the crowd of pleasure-seekers below seemed to mind. Or notice. Lean tan young bodies, of either sex, their privates covered by a slash or two of cloth, basked in the flickering glow of the torch lamps surrounding the pool. Some of them lounged on towels and sun chairs as if the full moon, which I could see reflected in the shimmery green water of the pool, was going to add to their already berry-brown complexions. Others romped, running around the pool's edge or in the water splashing, perpetual twelve-year-olds seeking perpetual summer.

I watched one well-endowed young woman tire of playing water baby with a boyfriend, climb out of the pool, tugging casually at her flimsy top which had slipped down to reveal dark half-circles of nipple. She was laughing, tossing back a headful of wet dark blond hair, shoving at the brawny chest of the guy who was climbing out of the pool after her. He pretended to be overpowered by her nudge and waved his arms and made a show of falling back in, but she no longer seemed amused.

She wasn't beautiful, exactly. The girl in the bedroom behind me was more classically beautiful, with a perfect,

high-cheekboned fashion model face and a slim but we
proportioned figure. A lot of the girls at this place (whic
was an apartment complex for so-called "swinging singles")
were the model type; others were more All-American-
style beauties, sunny-faced girls sung about in songs by
the Beach Boys. She fit neither type.

Her face was rather long, her nose long and narrow,
her eyes having an almost Oriental slant to them. Her
mouth was wide and when she smiled, gums showed.
Her figure was wrong, too: she was tall, at least an inch
taller than my five ten, with much too lanky a frame for
those huge breasts. Put that all together and she should
have been a goddamn freak.

But she wasn't. The big breasts rode firm and high;
she carried them well. Her face was unique-looking. You
might say haunting. The eyes especially, which were dark
blue with flecks of gold. Her voice was unusual, too—a
rich baritone as deep as a man's, as deep as mine, in fact
—but for some reason it only made her seem all the more
feminine.

I didn't know her, but I knew who she was. I was here
because of her. I'd been here, watching her, for almost a
week now. If she noticed me, she gave no indication. Not
that it mattered. The beard and mustache, once shaved off,
would make me someone else; when we met in another
context, one day soon, she'd have little chance of recog-
nizing me, even if she had managed to pick me out of this
crowd (which incidentally included several other beards
and plenty of mustaches, despite the unspoken rule that

ants were to be on the clean-cut side in appearance, if
ot in behavior).

I hoped I wouldn't have to kill her. I probably would.
But I hoped not. I wasn't crazy about killing a woman,
only that wasn't the problem. I hadn't counted on her
looking like this. Her picture had made her look almost
homely. I'd had no idea she radiated this aura of some
goddamn thing or another, some damn thing that made
me want to know her, made me uncomfortable at the
thought of having to kill her.

"Hey," she said.

I turned.

This one's name was Nancy. She was wearing a skimpy
black bikini. She had short dark black hair and looked
like a fashion model. Or did I mention that already?

"You want to go down and swim?" she asked.

"Later," I said.

"Is that Coke good?"

"It's fine."

"How come you don't drink anything but Coke and
that? Got something against liquor?"

"No. I have a mixed drink sometimes."

"What d'you come out here for?"

"It's nice out here."

"Is it because you knew I'd smoke?"

"I guess."

"Don't you have a single fucking vice?"

"Not one."

"Tell me something."

"Okay."

"You always this blue after you do it?"

"Just sometimes."

"Every time. With me, anyway. You always get all, uh, what's a good word for it?"

"Quiet."

"No. Morose. That's the word I want."

"Quiet is what I get. Don't read anything into anything, Nancy."

"I knew a guy like you once. He always got…quiet… after doing it."

"Is that right."

"You know what he said once?"

"No."

"He said, 'Doing it is like Christmas: after all the presents are open, you can't remember what the fuss was all about.'" And she laughed, but it got caught in her throat.

"What are you depressed for?"

"I'm not depressed. Don't read anything into anything, Burt."

Burt is the name I was using here. I thought it sounded like a good swinging singles name.

"My husband used to get sad, sometimes, after we did it."

Him again. She talked about him all the time, her ex. About what a son of a bitch he was, mostly. He was an English professor at some eastern university, with rich parents who underwrote him. He (or rather they) paid for Nancy's apartment here in Florida. There was a kid, too, a daughter I think, living with Nancy's parents in Michigan.

"You know what he used to say?" she asked.

"Something about Christmas?"

"No. He used to say that in France coming is called the little death."

"That's a little over my head, Nancy."

"Well, he was an intellectual. The lousy prick. But I think what it means is when you come, it's like dying for a second, you're going out of this life into some place different. You're not thinking about money or your problems or anything. All you can think of is coming. And you aren't thinking about that, either. You're just coming."

Down by the pool, the girl I'd come here to watch was sitting along the edge, kicking at the water, while her blond boyfriend tried to kid her out of her mood.

Nancy's hand was on my shoulder. I looked at her and she was lifting her mouth up to me, which meant I was supposed to kiss her, and I did. I put my hand between her legs and nudged her with a finger.

"Bang," I said.

She took my arm and pulled me into the bedroom.

2

We went down for a swim afterwards. I let Nancy do the swimming. I like to swim, but I don't like crowds. You can't swim in a crowd. All you can do is wade around bumping into people. So Nancy swam and I watched.

I didn't watch Nancy, though. I just pretended to. What my eyes were really on was the young woman with the big breasts and Oriental eyes and muscle-bound boyfriend. The boyfriend had the look of a Hollywood glamour boy gone slightly to seed. Thinning hair; puffy face; on the road to a paunch.

She was bored with him. He'd given up trying to talk her out of her indifference to him and was sitting in a beach chair with a drink in his hands, watching a blonde in a yellow bikini who sat across the way looking as bored with her companion as the big-breasted Oriental-eyed girl was bored with him.

I was bored, too. I hadn't been here a week and I was suffocating. I live in Wisconsin, near the Lake Geneva vacation center, and the summer months around those parts are cherished and enjoyed and, in the freezing cold winter months, looked forward to. I'd come here expecting a similar attitude. Instead I found the year-round summer was not so much taken for granted as squandered. Made meaningless.

I never imagined yards of beautiful exposed flesh under sunny skies could get dull. I never thought cool evenings full of cool drinks and warm glances could grow monotonous. I never dreamed sex could become so tedious.

Nancy wanted it every time I turned around. Three or four times a day, and the first couple days I was glad to accommodate. I'd gone for months without getting laid, and was more than ready. But after close to a week of it, I was just plain tired. The crazy part was what Nancy told me about the breakup of her marriage: "The son of a bitch was a sex maniac....He didn't respect me as a person at all." She told me this while we were taking a shower together.

All of this was new to me. I had never had to maintain a relationship with one woman while watching another woman I would most likely have to kill. I was used to keeping those two particular compartments of my life separate. I led a relatively normal social life in Wisconsin, including an occasional Nancy. But the life away from home was something else again. The business part of my life, I mean. The killing.

Of course I was in a different business now; slightly different, anyway. A new, self-created business that would require an intermixing, now and then, of the social me and the other one.

And I was finding out now, in my first time out, that playing both roles at once could prove to be a little disturbing.

Or anyway, irritating.

Though considering the boredom of this would-be paradise, a touch of irritation was maybe a good thing. At least I was awake. Aware, always, I was here on business. Perhaps I should've been thankful I hadn't been seduced by the sex-and-sun, flesh-and-fun atmosphere of the place.

Only I was finding something else irritating. Or disturbing, anyway. I had developed a nagging fascination with the woman I was watching, that Oriental-eyed woman with the big breasts, a woman who didn't seem to quite fit in here, and that fascination was unhealthy as hell, especially since this was my first outing in my new (make that revised) line of work.

How much longer was I going to have to watch her? Another week? A month? Longer? I never have liked stakeout work, and this swinging singles lifestyle, with its fringe "benefit" of constant sex, seemed likely to kill me before I had a chance to kill anybody myself.

Maybe tonight would be different. After all, the afternoon had been different. The tall, busty woman I'd been watching these past few days had acted a little strange this afternoon. All week she'd been giddy, just another bubble-headed fun-seeker playing footsy and everything-elsey with her blond boyfriend. But this afternoon she'd gotten moody. Her face had taken on an almost grim look. Her efforts at having fun seemed just that: efforts. Efforts that had failed and lapsed into…what? Depression? No. More like seriousness. A serious mood, rather than a black or bitchy one.

Something was up, maybe.

Not me, certainly: I was wilted. Nancy was going to have to learn to respect me as a person—for the rest of the night, anyway.

Meanwhile the crowd in and around the pool was beginning to thin. Nancy begged off around two-thirty and by that time there was only half a dozen of us left. My dragon lady was one. Her blond hunk of manhood was another, only now he was in the water with a blond hunk of womanhood whose own hunk she had managed to lose, along with the top of her bikini, and two small but perfectly shaped boobs bobbled in the water like apples, pink apples, if there is such a thing, or even if there isn't. I didn't much care either way. I was too wrung out to care. Not so the two blonds: they climbed out of the pool giggling and one chased the other into the shadows.

That left me alone with her.

Which was not good. A harmless conversation, idly struck…and the ballgame was over. Of course there was a whole pool between us; better an ocean. I needed to stay just some anonymous bearded guy who she had never really looked at close, otherwise the entire deal was blown.

But she wasn't looking at me. She was looking at the water. Staring at it, the surface rippling with the slight breeze, the torch lights shimmering eerily in reflection.

And then she got up and went up the open stairway to the second level, where her apartment was.

I stayed behind. I was, to say the least, relieved. And now that I had the pool to myself, I could have a nice, private swim, which is a daily ritual of mine, whenever possible, anyway.

I dove in.

I'd just swum my sixth easy lap when she came down wearing a dark, mannish pants suit, suitcase in either hand, and headed into the parking lot, from which, moments later, came the sound of squealing tires.

3

I could have followed her. I had my car keys in the pocket of my robe, which was with my towel, under the beach chair where I'd been sitting before I started my swim.

But I might have looked just a shade conspicuous jumping into the Opel GT soaking wet, in nothing but a pair of swim trunks, and considering I was already afraid she might have taken some notice of me, following her, at this moment, in my present condition, didn't seem, well, prudent.

The next best thing to following her was to find out where she was going.

So that's what I decided to do. Try to do, anyway.

I hadn't ever gotten in her apartment to look around, despite the number of days I'd been there. She hadn't left the grounds of the place since I'd arrived: she sent her boyfriend out to do the grocery shopping, and with all the drinking and sex available on the premises, who needed to go out for anything except supplies?

I maybe could have got in and searched her place while she was down by the pool with her blond plaything; she did spend a lot of time down there, after all. But who was to say when she or the plaything might tire of the pool and come up for a nap or something. And, too, during all but a few of the nocturnal hours, I was playing play-thing myself, for Nancy, so when the fuck was I supposed to get in that apartment for a look?

Now.

Now I could do it. The dragon lady was gone, packed and left in the middle of the night, as a matter of fact, and her boyfriend was apparently shacked up, at least temporarily, with a new mistress…and I don't mean mistress in the modern sense, not exactly.

I mean mistress in the dictionary sense, "woman in authority, in control." Women ruled at that place. It should've been called the Amazon Arms (and not Beach Shore Apartments, which is redundant as hell, I know, but then the owner/manager's name was Bob Roberts, so you figure it). The Beach Shore rented exclusively to women. Divorced women, mostly, alimony-rich divorced women.

All the rooms had double beds, and there were a lot of men around, but the men would come and go, so to speak, and the women stayed on.

Which is why it hadn't been hard to infiltrate the place. I just dropped in one afternoon and sat by the pool, wearing my tight little trunks, and waited to be picked up. It wasn't as degrading as I'd imagined it, but it was degrading enough. As any woman reading this could tell you.

So now that the dragon lady was away, with an apparent rift developed between her and her plaything, I figured I'd find that apartment very empty. And the risk of being interrupted while I had my look around was little or no.

Getting in would be no problem. Getting in was never a problem around this place, in about any sense you can think of. The asshole who managed the place (the owner, old Bob Roberts, remember?) was never in his own apartment, as he considered that part of his function was servicing any of his tenants who were momentarily between playthings. He liked to tell his tenants his door was always open, and it was. So was his fly.

Anyway, I walked in one afternoon, found his master key in a drawer and took it to a Woolworth's in the nearby good-size town, where I had a dupe made, returned his key, and got back in bed with Nancy, all in the course of fifty minutes.

I used to be good at picking locks, but got out of the habit. For what I'd been doing the past few years, I'd seldom needed tools of that sort, as most of my work was in the Midwest, where security tends to be lax, where most doors can be opened with a credit card, and there are lots of other ways to get in a place if you have to, easier ways than picking a lock, I mean, which honest-to-Christ requires daily practice. Anybody tells you picking locks is easy is somebody who doesn't know how to pick locks.

I got out of the pool.

I put on my robe, went up the steps and inside, where I found the corridor empty and felt no apprehension at all as I worked the dupe of the owner/manager's master key in the lock and went in. I turned on the lights (the windows of her apartment faced the ocean-front side of the building, so no one was likely to see them on, and even so, so what?) and began poking around.

The apartment itself was identical in layout to Nancy's, except backwards, as this was on the opposite side of the hall. The decorating was very different, which surprised me: apparently each tenant could have her own decorating done, so where a wall in Nancy's had pastel blue wallpaper, light color blue like Wisconsin summer sky, the dragon lady had shiny metallic silver wallpaper; other walls were standard dark paneling in either apartment, but in this one, for example, a gleaming metal bookcase-cum-knickknack rack jutted across the living room, cutting it in half, with few books on it and a lot of weird African-looking statues and some abstract sculptures made of glazed black something. And where in Nancy's place there was a lot of wood, nothing furniture, everything antiques, this place had plastic furniture, metal furniture, glass furniture, all of it looking expensive and cheap at the same time.

In the bedroom, above the round waterbed, with its white silk sheets and black furry spread, was a painting. A black square with an immense red dot all but engulfing it. Nancy had a picture above her bed, too. An art nouveau print of a beautiful woman in a flowing scarf against a pastel background. Nancy had an antique brass bed. I had the feeling these girls weren't two of a kind.

Meanwhile, I was going through things. The name she was using here was Glenna Cole, but I found identification cards of various sorts in several other names. The

Broker's name for her was Ivy. Knowing Broker's so-called sense of humor, that probably came from poison ivy. Broker called me Quarry. Because (he said) a quarry is carved out of rock. The Broker's dead now.

I found a gun. A spare, probably. She wouldn't have taken her suitcases with her unless she was going off on a job. That was my guess, anyway, and it came from experience. Also, the gun was just a little purse thing, a pearl-handled .22 automatic, and I imagined she used something a little heavier than that in her work. A .38, at least. Speaking of which, I did find a box of .38 shells behind some lacy panties in a drawer, and that substantiated my guesswork, as there was no gun here that went with these shells.

What I didn't find was evidence of where she'd gone. I went through the wastebaskets, and I even went through a bag of garbage in her kitchen, and found nothing, no plane or bus reservation notice, no nothing. I even played the rubbing a pencil against the top blank sheet of a note-pad trick, and while it seems to work on television, all I got for my trouble was dirty fingers.

I sat on an uncomfortable-looking comfortable couch in her living room and wondered what to do next.

That was when her boyfriend came in.

4

I said, "Who the hell are you?"

His mouth dropped open like a trap door.

"So who the hell are you?" I demanded again.

He cocked his head like a dog trying to comprehend its master, narrowing his eyes, making them seem more close-set than they really were.

"Well?" I said.

That's the only way I know to handle a situation like that: turn the tables, put the shoe on the other foot, or whatever other cliche you want to use to describe what I was doing to him. It was the only way I knew that might avoid immediate violence. I don't care for physical violence myself, and try to duck it whenever possible.

Especially when faced with a guy both bigger and stronger than me, facts made obvious by his standing there in swim trunks and towel, the latter flung casually over a classically muscular shoulder.

"Well, are you coming in or aren't you?" I asked.

He pushed the door shut. His teeth were showing. He wasn't smiling. But he was too confused to be violent. At the moment.

"I don't know you," he said.

"If I knew you," I said, "would I be asking your god-damn name every couple seconds?"

His eyebrows were as light a blond as the hair on his head. His nose was small, almost feminine. He really was prettier-looking than the dragon lady. But nowhere near as interesting.

"You got a reason for being in Glenna's room?" he said. His voice was medium range, flat, uninteresting.

"Sure. Do you?"

"Yeah. Yeah, I do. I live here."

"The hell you say." I knew he did, of course, had seen the men's clothing in the closet and in dresser drawers, and knew of the female domination of the place which meant any man here was living with whatever woman he served. What I didn't know was how fast this asshole was, that he'd pull a wham/bam/thank-you-ma'am on that female counterpart of himself he'd gone off into the shadows with. I mean, even at the Beach Shore you spent the night with whoever you banged. Sometimes you stayed the month.

"Hey," he said, sitting in a chair across from me, a glass coffee table separating us. "Hey, I've seen you some-place. You staying here with somebody? Have I seen you down by the pool?"

"I'm staying here. You might have seen me."

"But we haven't met."

"That's right."

"I'm Norm Morrow."

"Burt Thompson."

We didn't shake hands, by the way.

"Okay, then. Okay, Burt. Now we're introduced. Now maybe you don't mind going into what you're doing in here?"

"I'm waiting for Glenna."

"Glenna's gone."

"She'll be back."

"Not for a while, bud."

"I'll wait a while. And it's Burt."

"I don't give a fuck it's Henry Kissinger. I'm starting to get the idea you're fucking around with me, and I don't like it."

"If you hadn't gone fucking around with some other piece of ass but Glenna, maybe she wouldn't have asked me up here."

"That's horseshit, pal."

"How so?"

"Glenna doesn't give a damn what I do while she's gone, she's gone sometimes a month at a time, and she doesn't expect me to be a fucking priest, you know? It's an understanding we got. And I'm beginning to understand something else…I had about enough of you. Now what is this *really* about?"

"All I know is she asked me up, asked me to stay on, maybe she just figured I'd pass the word on to you your welcome was worn out…"

"Hey. You were just leaving, sport."

"I don't want any trouble. You're a whole lot stronger than me, I can see that. No need to go proving it."

"So get the fuck out of here, then."

"Look, why don't we just ask Glenna which of us she wants to hang around."

"What? She split, she's gone, hasn't that sunk in yet, you jackass?"

"We'll call her and ask her."

"I don't have a number to reach her, and neither do you."

"I admit I don't. I just thought maybe you did. You say you live here."

"Well…sometimes she leaves a number."

"Yeah?"

"I don't know why I'm playing along with you on this, I really don't…"

"We'll call. Come on."

"She won't be there till tomorrow, at least. She's driving, and it's a long way where she's headed."

"Where's that?"

"You're her new boyfriend and you don't know? Hey. That's all. That's all I can take. Just haul your ass off that couch and get outa here. Okay?"

I was admiring a metallic abstract sculpture on the glass coffee table between us. It was egg-shaped, the sculpture, with an indentation on either side, and about the size of a baseball, a little taller maybe. When I hit him with it, he went down without a sound. He missed the table, landed soft on the tufts of shag carpet. I hit him again, once, in the same spot, and made sure the skull was cracked open.

One good thing was he landed on his right side and it was his left side I'd hit, the left side of his head I mean, so there wasn't any blood on the carpet, and wouldn't be if I moved him quick and careful.

I left him in the bathtub, after pulling off his trunks, heaving him in, turning on the shower, and leaving him looking like he'd slipped and fallen in there, cracking his head open against the side of the tub.

The work of art I wrapped in a towel and took with me, for later disposal.

The telephone number she left him I found under the phone.

Quarry's Story Continues
In Thrilling New Novels

THE FIRST QUARRY

by MAX ALLAN COLLINS

QUARRY'S FIRST ASSIGNMENT!

Where did Quarry's story start? For the first time ever, the best-selling author of ROAD TO PERDITION takes us back to the beginning, revealing the never-before-told story of Quarry's first job: infiltrating a college town and eliminating a professor whose affair with one of his beautiful, young students is the least of his sins...

PRAISE FOR MAX ALLAN COLLINS

"Max Allan Collins is the closest thing we have to a 21st-century Mickey Spillane and...will please any fan of old-school, hardboiled crime fiction."
— This Week

"Collins has an outwardly artless style that conceals a great deal of art."
— New York Times

"No one can twist you through a maze with as much intensity and suspense as Max Allan Collins."
— Clive Cussler

**Available now from your favorite bookseller.
For more information, visit
www.HardCaseCrime.com**

Quarry's Story Continues
In Thrilling New Novels

QUARRY'S
CHOICE

by MAX ALLAN COLLINS

QUARRY TAKES ON THE DIXIE MAFIA

Quarry is a pro in the murder business. When the man he works for becomes a target himself, Quarry is sent South to remove a traitor in the ranks. But in this wide-open city—with sin everywhere, and betrayal around every corner—Quarry must make the most dangerous choice of his deadly career: *who to kill?*

PRAISE FOR MAX ALLAN COLLINS

*"Collins breaks out a really good one,
knocking over the hard-boiled competition
(Parker and Leonard for sure, maybe even Puzo)
with a one-two punch: a feisty storyline told
bittersweet and wry…the book is
unputdownable. Never done better."*
— Kirkus Reviews

"An exceptional storyteller."
— San Diego Union Tribune

*"Rippling with brutal violence and
surprising sexuality…I savored every turn."*
— Bookgasm

**Available now from your favorite bookseller.
For more information, visit
www.HardCaseCrime.com**